MURDER AT THE CLINIC

A Midwest Cozy Mystery - Book 2

BY

DIANNE HARMAN

Published by: Dianne Harman
www.dianneharman.com

Interior, cover design and website by
Vivek Rajan
www.RewireYourDNA.com

ISBN: 978-1537621456

CONTENTS

ACKNOWLEDGMENTS

Thank you for taking the time to read this book. I've told my readers before how much I enjoy writing, but having readers like my books is the icing on the cake!

This is book number two in the popular Midwest Cozy Mystery Series featuring Kat Denham, also known as the writer, Sexy Cissy. If you like it, you might enjoy the books in my other four cozy mystery series, Cedar Bay, Liz Lucas, High Desert, and Jack Trout. Because of you, every one of my books has received Amazon's prestigious "bestseller" gold banner, and as I'm writing this, two of them currently have the coveted banner next to their titles. I feel so lucky to be the author whose books have received this recognition. Again, thank you!

I'm often asked how I come up with ideas for my books. Even I have to admit the idea for this one was unique. I was at my acupuncturist's clinic receiving a treatment for my chronic low back pain – a result of too many hours writing at my computer – when a thought came to me and I asked my doctor, "What would happen if…?" He looked at me and said, "In twenty years, no patient of mine has ever even thought of something like that. You're not normal." I told him I thought normalcy was a highly overrated attribute, and so this book was born!

I've been going to Dr. Lam off and on for twenty years and have always had great results. It's well worth the thirty minute drive from my home to his office in Buena Park, California. Here's his website if you ever get to that neck of the woods and have a health issue: http://www.eliteprofessionalmedical.com.

As always, thanks to Vivek Rajan, who I depend on for creating the wonderful covers for my books as well as preparing them for publication. And I would be remiss without giving my husband, Tom, a huge shout out for his unfailing cheerleading and vigilant eye for manuscript mistakes. To say I'm grateful to them would be a total understatement. Thanks to both of you for making my work look good!

And as I usually do, a verbal ear scratch for my dog Kelly, for maintaining her place at my feet while I'm writing and her need for physical exercise which makes me take a break once in a while from my computer. Thanks, Kelly!

Lastly, if you would like to read something a little different from my cozy mysteries, you might want to try the Teddy Saga, two books about politics. Some of you know that I spent twelve years in Sacramento, California, when my husband was in the Legislature, so a lot that's in those books is "inside baseball." I have also authored the Coyote Series, three books of international psychological suspense. The first one, Blue Coyote Motel, was the recipient of a number of awards. Enjoy!

Kindle & Ebooks for FREE

Go to www.dianneharman.com/freepaperback.html and get your FREE copies of Dianne's books and Dianne's favorite recipes immediately by signing up for her newsletter.

Once you've signed up for her newsletter you're eligible to win a Kindle. One lucky winner is picked every week. Hurry before the offer ends!

CHAPTER ONE

Kat Denham walked up the steps of the country club and stood at the top for a moment, breathing in the scents of the warm spring day. She loved the seasons in the Midwest, even the hot summers and cold winter months, but there was something special about Spring. She inhaled deeply and let the earthy smell of the freshly mowed golf course grass fill her nostrils. The club gardening crew had planted hundreds of spring bulbs which provided a riot of color that lined the steps and overflowed the raised planters surrounding the front of the clubhouse.

The woman she was meeting for lunch, her acupuncturist, Mitzi Green, didn't know it, but today was a special day for Kat. She'd just finished writing her tenth novel and had dropped the manuscript off at the home of Bev Simpson, her friend and editor, to read. Although her novel writing had been a leap of faith in the beginning, she now had a solid following of loyal readers who looked forward to each of her new releases.

"Hello, Mrs. Denham. It's good to see you. Involved in solving any murders today?" Barbara, the affable dining room hostess, asked as Kat walked over to her. Barbara's allusion to murder brought back the memory of when Kat discovered the body of her then editor, Nancy Jennings, and Kat was forced to find the murderer before she became the next victim.

Being the author of steamy romance novels written under the pen name of Sexy Cissy at first had been a liability when the local residents of her small Kansas college town discovered that Kat and Sexy Cissy were one and the same. However, it all seemed to change when she succeeded in catching the murderer who had killed Nancy Jennings. Once that happened, things began to return to normal. Even her daughter, Lacie, had accepted the fact her mother was the very successful Sexy Cissy.

It didn't seem to have affected her relationship with the handsome district attorney, who was more than happy to spend time with someone who wrote sexy novels. She smiled wryly at his ongoing suggestion that their relationship should move on to the next stage. Widowed, in her fifties, and having been out of the dating scene for a long time, she wasn't sure just how that was supposed to happen. He always laughed when they talked about her books, and he constantly reminded her that anyone with her imagination, if that's what it was, should have no problem taking their relationship to the next level.

"The answer to your question, Barbara, is a resounding no, and believe me, I'm glad to be able to say that. I'm meeting Mitzi Green for lunch. Is she here yet?"

"She got here a few minutes ago. She's at the table at the far end of the dining room. I didn't think you'd want to sit at or near that dining room table where the whole mystery of the Jennings murder began, so I decided to put you there."

"Thanks, Barbara, that was very thoughtful. I appreciate it, and you're absolutely right. I really would prefer to forget that whole experience. See you later."

"Here's today's menu. I need to seat the group that just walked in," Barbara said as she handed Kat a menu.

Kat threaded her way through the maze of tables in the dining room, glad that Mitzi had thought to make a reservation. For some reason Mondays at the country club were always busy, and today was no different. She saw Mitzi waving to her and smiling broadly as Kat approached the table. Mitzi stood up and Kat gave her a big hug and then she sat down across from her. When she saw the champagne filled glass in front of her place setting Kat asked, "How did you know?"

"Know what?" Mitzi asked.

"That I finished my tenth book early this morning and dropped it off at my editor's home on the way here. Why, isn't that what we're celebrating?"

"Well, we certainly can celebrate that, but it wasn't why I wanted to meet you for lunch today. There's something else I'd like to celebrate," Mitzi answered with a smile.

"Other than the fact that we're probably celebrating your loss of the last ten pounds you've been trying to lose for the last year, I'm clueless."

Mitzi picked up her champagne flute and said, "Kat, please pick yours up. Okay, here goes. I'm getting married. I'd like you to be my matron of honor. Will you?"

Kat sat with her raised champagne glass in her hand, unable to speak, her mouth hanging unattractively open. Finally, she recovered and said, "First of all, yes. Second of all, who is he? And thirdly, I've never been so happy for anyone in my life. Now, tell me everything."

Mitzi Green and Kat Denham had been friends since college. Even then, Mitzi had been overweight, actually very overweight. She'd never married and had worked as a librarian for many years. When she turned forty-five she had what some would call a mid-life crisis. For Mitzi, it meant that her dabbling for years in Eastern philosophies and Eastern medicine culminated in her decision to become an acupuncturist. The university in the small college town where they lived had recently added a Doctor of Acupuncture and Oriental Medicine to their curriculum, and Mitzi had quit her job at the library in order to become a full time student there.

She'd flourished in her studies, and the department had been so impressed with her academic record that when she graduated they offered her a job teaching acupuncture at the university. Along with her morning teaching job, the department gave her permission to treat private patients as well as have the level one interns observe her acupuncture treatments. She also oversaw the level two interns who provided acupuncture treatments to people who came to the department to obtain free treatment for a variety of physical problems.

During her career reinvention, Mitzi decided to reinvent herself as well. Having taken a number of classes in oriental medicine, she applied what she'd learned and for the last few years had slowly and methodically lost one hundred fifty pounds. A year earlier she'd undergone surgery to remove the excess skin resulting from the dramatic weight loss.

Kat smiled at the beautiful woman sitting across the table from her who bore no resemblance to the woman she'd known for years except for the large hazel eyes that never missed anything. In addition to the skin removal, Mitzi had undergone a facelift and an eyelift.

Never having worn makeup in the past, the term mousy librarian, no, make that fat mousy librarian, described her perfectly. Now she was an expert at applying makeup. Her creamy complexion set off those unforgettable eyes which had been enhanced with perfectly applied eye shadow and liner. French tip fingernails and toenails spoke to the extent of the change in Mitzi Green. Her light brown hair was subtly woven with blond highlights. Quite simply, Mitzi Green had become drop-dead gorgeous.

Kat had never been jealous of Mitzi's redo. While Kat knew she was definitely getting older, since face and body maintenance took a little longer each day than it used to, with her big blue eyes, blond hair, and a figure that still commanded attention, she was very secure with how she looked. Although some would say she was aging gracefully, at times Kat called it a big pain in the neck!

CHAPTER TWO

"I'm not the least bit surprised some man wants to make you his wife. It's about time you were discovered," Kat said, "but you've never mentioned anything about him to me. Who is he? What does he do? Where does he live? When's the wedding?"

"Whoa, Kat. Let me start from the beginning. I still can't believe all this is happening to me, Fat Mitzi."

"Mitzi, those days are long gone. Look at you now!"

Just then the waiter walked over to their table. "Have you made your decisions, ladies?" he asked. They gave him their orders, and Kat continued.

"I never want to hear that name again. It's a name from the past for someone who no longer exists. Look what you've done with your life. I'm so proud of you, and I'm so happy for you."

"Okay, his name is Rex Brown. He's a doctor, a plastic surgeon, and we met when I was his patient."

"Mitzi, I thought doctors weren't supposed to develop personal relationships with their patients. Are you sure that was a wise thing to do, even though it's probably too late now? And it makes me a little nervous about him. Sorry, but that's just how I feel."

"That's okay, Kat. As I understand it, ethically doctors aren't supposed to develop relationships with patients they are presently treating. Rex called me after he'd finished treating me, and asked me out to dinner. As you know, my life has not been one of dates and dinners. I was so scared I didn't know how to answer him. On some level, I think he understood. He asked for my address and said he'd pick me up the following evening, and that I should dress casually. I really never had a chance to say yes or no. Don't forget, the man has seen me at my worst. Well, maybe not my worst, because I'd lost almost all of my weight when I went to him for surgery, but there was a whole lot of excess skin just hanging on my body."

"Mitzi, this is so romantic. You know you're going to be an inspiration for every woman who knows you, both for having a first marriage at this stage of your life and for achieving a major weight loss."

A shadow crossed Mitzi's face, and she said, "I think there are a few people who wish I'd never changed. I'd put Rex's ex-fiancée at the top of the list. Don't think she was too thrilled to lose out to Fat Mitzi. Another one who's not real thrilled with the new me is a Vietnamese doctor at the university. Actually he's just not pleased with me, period, neither the new me nor the old me. He's in my department, and we're both being considered for the position of Assistant Dean of the Acupuncture Department. It's a pretty big deal. He and I were students together, and we got along alright then, but with the weight loss and everything else, I get the distinct feeling he wishes I would just go away, so he can become the assistant dean."

"I'm sure there are some people who would have preferred it if you'd simply stayed just like you were. Often when people change for the better, they become a threat. Looks like that's true in your case. On one hand you're a romantic threat, and on the other hand, you're a professional threat, but look at it this way, before those changes, you weren't a threat to anyone! Think most people would take being a threat over not being a threat, if it meant an improvement in their lifestyle."

"That's probably true, but it would be nice if everyone was just as happy for me as I am. I suppose that could only happen in a perfect world, and from what I've seen, a perfect world doesn't exist."

She was interrupted by the waiter who served a large salad to Mitzi with oil and vinegar on the side. He served Kat the special of the day, braised short ribs over bleu cheese mashed potatoes. "Sorry, Mitzi," Kat said. "I hope this doesn't bother you, but I can't pass up short ribs. They're one of my favorites."

"Not in the least. Believe it or not, I've gotten to like rabbit food. Actually, I've been using a type of psychological behavioral conditioning, and I've learned how to convince myself that if I eat something like that, I'll become sick."

Kat put down her fork and said in a concerned voice, "Mitzi, please tell me your weight loss didn't happen because you've become bulimic."

Mitzi laughed and said, "Kat, you know me. Even when I'm sick I'll walk around for hours before I'll throw up. I've been known to deliberately hold my head up so I won't throw up. I'll do anything not to. That's why this particular type of mind exercise works so well for me. I've convinced myself that I'll throw up if I eat fattening things, and since I'll do anything to avoid that, it makes it easy for me to stay away from those things."

"All right. Let's change the subject. Have you decided on a date for the wedding? Has Rex been married before? Are you going to be a stepmother? I'll let you take a bite of your salad before you answer," Kat said as she took a bite of her entrée. She decided it would be unwise to tell Mitzi just how good it was.

"Okay, Kat," Mitzi said after she'd sampled her salad. We're getting married in late July. You can drop the surprised look on your face. I know it's only two months away, but at our age, and he's a little older than I am, what are we waiting for?"

"Actually, I think that's smart. Tell me more."

"In answer to your questions, Rex has never been married, and he has no children. He's told me he was married to his work until he met me, although he was recently engaged. I'm glad he doesn't have any children, because I've heard horror stories of relationships between stepmothers and stepchildren. I'm glad I won't have to go through that."

"Me, too. Where are you going to be married?" Kat asked.

"Well, that's one of the reasons I wanted to have lunch with you."

"I'm confused. What are you talking about?"

Mitzi took a deep breath and said, "Kat, you know how much I love your house and your beautiful back yard. Rex and I've decided to have a small, intimate wedding," she said as she began to speak rapidly, "And I was hoping we could be married in your back yard and have the reception at your house. Of course, I'll take care of all of the costs like the flowers, the catering, etcetera. What do you think?"

"I think I'm in shock, Mitzi. I'm flattered you like my house and garden that much, but are you sure you want to be married there?"

"If it's all right with you, yes. Obviously I talked to Rex about it, and he thinks it's a wonderful idea. By the way, he plays golf with Blaine, so he feels like he knows you. I was actually thinking I could have the country club cater the reception. Well, what do you say?"

"I'd be honored," Kat said. "Of course I'll need to spruce up the garden a bit, but Jose can take care of that. Naturally, I'll need the exact date. Have you gotten a wedding dress? What do you want me to wear? Are you going to have any bridesmaids?"

"Sounds schmaltzy, but since I've never been married, I wanted to be married in white. I bought a silk cream-colored wedding dress last weekend at the County Club Plaza in Kansas City. I got it at that fancy wedding shop that's practically an institution there. Cost me an arm and a leg, but I figure, what am I saving it for? I've decided not to have any bridesmaids. As I said, it's going to be a small wedding. Since each of us is an only child and our parents are deceased, our families consist of some cousins who neither one of is close with. We both have friends and some professional colleagues we'll invite, but that's about it."

Kat's head was churning with everything that needed to be done before the wedding. She'd been thinking about getting a couple of new pieces of furniture and decided having the wedding at her home was just the push she needed to finally do it. She didn't bother to tell Mitzi, knowing it would make her feel guilty.

"Whoops," Mitzi said as she looked at her watch. "I've got to run. I need to get back to work to oversee some interns and see patients. Would you sign the bill for me? My club number is 316. We'll talk more tomorrow. I think your appointment's at ten in the morning. See you then, and thanks for being such a good friend."

Kat motioned for the waiter to bring the check, and she wrote down their names and their club numbers. She'd just finished when Barbara walked over to the table.

"That was Mitzi Green wasn't it, the one everyone used to call Fat Mitzi." Barbara said.

"Yes, she's lost a lot of weight, and pretty much changed her appearance. I think she's gorgeous. What do you think?"

"I couldn't agree more. She's had a social membership at the club for years, but I haven't seen her here in a long time. She'd made a reservation under that name, but I really didn't pay much attention to it. I thought it was strange there would be two Mitzi Greens in a town this small, but sometimes those things happen. She's like the ugly duckling that's turned into a beautiful swan. Kat, I've got an idea. You're an author. Why don't you write a novel about a fat woman who becomes beautiful? Bet a lot of people could identify with that, or even wish it was them."

"Not a bad idea, Barbara. What you don't know is the swan is going to marry her Prince Charming, and in her case he turns out to be a doctor."

"See, that's even better. Readers would love it. A really happy ever after ending to a story. Bet that one would make the best seller list, for sure."

"Thanks for the suggestion, Barbara. You might be onto something. Tell you what, if I do write it, I'll credit you on the acknowledgment page for giving me the idea," she said laughing as she stood up to leave. "See you soon."

During her drive back home Kat's mind was whirling with thoughts about the wedding, but in spite of those thoughts, Barbara's words kept coming back to her. She'd been thinking for quite awhile it might be interesting to see if she could write a book that would sell in a genre other than steamy romance, and this might be her chance. She decided when she got home she'd do some research on the Internet and see what she could find out about acupuncturists. Maybe she could write a novel loosely based on an acupuncturist who was an ugly duckling and became a beautiful swan. The more she thought about it, the better she liked the idea.

Little did Kat know that the swan was about to become embroiled in a murder mystery, and it would be up to Kat to find the murderer in order to save both the swan and Kat.

CHAPTER THREE

Fortunately, the university where Mitzi taught and had her acupuncture practice was only ten minutes away from the country club. She parked in the doctor's private parking lot and hurried into the building where she oversaw her interns and treated patients.

"There you are," said Rochelle, the acupuncture clinic's receptionist. "The dean's office called, and Dr. Warren said he'd like to see you when you're finished this afternoon. He wanted me to call and confirm the time. I looked at your schedule, and it looks like you'll be finished at 4:30. Okay if I call him back and confirm that time? Also, your interns are waiting for you in your office."

Rochelle Salazar was in her third year of the acupuncture program at the university. When her children left for college, her husband decided the time had come to end the marriage, and he'd left as well. Although Rochelle had a college degree, she'd never worked, preferring to be a stay-at-home mom. She was ready for a change in her life and became a student in the acupuncture program. When it was announced there was an opening for a receptionist in the acupuncture clinic, she eagerly applied for it and was accepted. It also helped defray the cost of her tuition. She worked for Mitzi and one of the other professors, Dr. Binh Nguyen, who also treated patients and oversaw interns at the clinic.

There was no love lost between the two doctors of acupuncture, even less now that one of them would soon be named the assistant dean of the department. Dr. Nguyen made no secret of the fact he thought American women had no place working as acupuncturists, even though the majority of the students in the acupuncture curriculum at the university were women and definitely American.

Dr. Nguyen told whoever would listen to him that he'd been one of the top acupuncturists in Vietnam prior to coming to the United States. He told people he came from a long line of doctors of acupuncture, and also made it known he felt the education he'd received in Vietnam was far superior to what he'd received in the United States. The small university in Kansas had grandfathered in a few of the classes he'd taken in Vietnam, but even with his past experience he'd ended up spending three years taking classes in acupuncture at the university.

Every time Mitzi saw Dr. Nguyen she was reminded of a conversation she'd had with a woman over dinner at the local professional organization for acupuncturists. Even though it had happened over a year ago, Mitzi remembered it as if it had happened yesterday. When Dr. Nguyen had entered the room, the woman had said under her breath to Mitzi, "He likes to think he's such a big shot. I'm half tempted to tell everyone he couldn't even pass the licensing exam the first time around. He had to take it a second time. You sure don't see him bragging about that."

"Yes, Rochelle, please call Dr. Warren and tell him 4:30 will be fine. Anything else I need to know before I get started?"

Rochelle looked around and lowered her voice. "Dr. Green, there's something I think you need to know."

"What is it, Rochelle? Better hurry, because I'm running a little late as it is."

"You know how you and Dr. Nguyen share an office and each of you has your own desk in it?"

"Yes," Mitzi said impatiently glancing at her watch.

"Well, I usually eat my lunch in the cafeteria, but today, I needed to study some more before tomorrow's test. I brought a sandwich back from the cafeteria and saw Dr. Nguyen sitting at your desk, looking through the drawers. I didn't want him to know I'd seen him, so I quietly left and then made a big deal about noisily opening the door to the reception area. I stayed near the door for a minute or so, and when I got to my desk I looked in your office, and he was sitting at his own desk. He greeted me and said he hadn't realized how late it was, and he needed to leave because he was meeting a colleague for lunch. He was gone in a couple of minutes."

"Dr. Nguyen was going through my desk drawers? Why would he do that?" Mitzi asked in a confused voice.

"I have no idea, but my first reaction is that he'd love to get some information on you that wasn't favorable, so he'd be named as the assistant dean and not you. I never have trusted him."

"Since I don't think there's any information about me that's unfavorable, he may have to look for a long time. Thanks, Rochelle. I usually don't lock my desk, but I guess I better start. I really don't like someone going through it." She walked across the hall to her office and greeted the waiting interns.

Mitzi spent the afternoon walking from one treatment room to another making sure that the level one and two interns were carefully observing her as she inserted the acupuncture needles at the acupuncture points on the appropriate meridian lines for the ailment that was being treated. In return for free treatment the patients had to sign a release stating they had been told that while they would be treated by a licensed acupuncturist, the acupuncturist would be teaching interns during their treatment. Later in the semester, the interns would treat the patients, and Mitzi would be the one observing. Dr. Nguyen adhered to the same procedure on the days when he was working with his interns. Each of them had four interns per three-week period during the semester. The hands-on experience was a critically important part of their education.

At 4:30, after the last patient had left, and she'd said good-bye to her interns, Mitzi left for Dr. Warren's office, totally unprepared for what he was going to tell her.

CHAPTER FOUR

Mitzi walked next door to the building where Dr. Warren, the Dean of the Acupuncture Department, had his office, opened his office door, and warmly greeted his receptionist, Hannah. "It's good to see you again, Hannah, how are your classes coming along?"

"Absolutely great. As you know, I'm almost finished with the program, and the best news is I already have a job. Of course I have to pass the state board exam, but I think I will. My dad recently played golf with a doctor who has a medical practice in the Westport area of Kansas City. He's an orthopedist, and when he's finished with the surgery portion of his patient's treatment he likes to refer them to other members of his staff, for example, a physical therapist or a chiropractor. He's been looking for an acupuncturist for quite a while. He likes to offer a holistic approach to the patient's problems in addition to the more traditional types of treatment involving surgery."

"Congratulations. That's great. There's nothing better than being able to go into an established practice and get referrals. Consider yourself lucky."

"Believe me, I do. I'll tell Dr. Warren you're here."

A few moments later the door to Dr. Warren's office opened and he said, "Mitzi, please come in." He shut the door behind her and indicated she should sit in the chair across from him. "Thanks for coming. An issue has come up that I need to discuss with you."

"You sound so serious. What is it?"

"First of all, let me say that I've always thought your work was excellent."

Good grief, is he going to tell me he's naming Dr. Nguyen as his assistant dean? Is this the beginning of a "you lose" speech?

"Thank you, Dr. Warren. I believe in acupuncture, and I take my choice of a profession very seriously."

"I thought you did, too, Mitzi, and that's why I'm so troubled by what I'm about to say."

"I'm sorry, but I'm not following you."

"I don't blame you. I think I'm making a real mess of this, so let me just say it straight out. I've received information that several of your patients have told people they felt your treatment harmed them, rather than helped them." He sat back in his chair and folded his hands, waiting for her response.

Mitzi started to stand up, then sat back down. Her face became pale and try as she might, she couldn't stop the small tear that slipped from her right eye and lazily made its way down her cheek. After a few moments she said, "I'd like to know who told you that."

"I'm sorry, Mitzi, I can't say. I'm sure you understand that information of this type is confidential."

"No, as a matter of fact, I don't," she said as her voice rose in anger. "My reputation is on the line here, as well as my application to become your assistant dean. I think you owe me the courtesy of telling me where these untruths came from, and believe me, they are untruths. I've never had one complaint given to me in person or lodged against me since I started practicing acupuncture, and now out of the blue, you're telling me that several people think I've harmed them?" she asked incredulously. "And just how do you expect me to defend myself against accusations which are nothing more than a rumor if you won't tell me how you discovered this vicious allegation?"

"Mitzi, put yourself in my place. I would very much like to have you as my assistant, but when someone in my position receives information like this, I have no choice but to determine if there's any truth to it."

"I can understand that. Were you given the names of the people who supposedly made those claims?"

"No," he answered as he avoided looking her in the eye.

She stood up and began pacing back and forth. "And just how do you intend to find out whether or not it's the truth if you don't even know who said my treatment may have harmed them?"

"I don't have a plan in mind. When I was given this information, I hoped you might know of a disgruntled patient, and we could go from there."

"Wait, Doctor. You weren't told this? Is that what you're saying? That it came to you anonymously? And might I ask just how did you get the information?" she asked angrily.

He looked down at his hands and then towards the far side of the room, as if he couldn't look at her directly while he answered. "I returned from an early lunch meeting today, and there was a note on my desk with the information in question on it. I don't know who put it there. I asked Hannah if she knew anything about it, but she said she'd gone to the cafeteria for lunch and wasn't here during lunchtime. Several of the acupuncture teachers were having lunch in the lounge, so she didn't feel she needed to lock the door.

Mitzi sat back down in her chair. "Doctor, I want you to know how much I respect you, but I have to say it must have occurred to you when two people are being considered for the same position, and you just happen to receive negative information regarding one of them, that maybe, just maybe, the other person had something to do with it. Did that thought occur to you?"

"Of course it did. I know Dr. Nguyen can come off as brilliant and arrogant at times, but I've never known him to do something like this. Have you?"

"No, but I sure wouldn't put it past him. He's made no bones to a number of people that American women belong in front of the kitchen stove or washing machine, rather than an acupuncture treatment table. I really have nothing further to say, Doctor. I believe my professional record speaks for itself, but if you choose to believe gossip by unnamed persons, I'm not sure I'd want to work for you anyway." She stormed out of his office and slammed the door behind her.

"Dr. Green, is anything…"

Hannah never finished her sentence, because Mitzi was on her way to the parking lot, thinking very uncharitable thoughts about one Dr. Binh Nguyen. All she wanted to do was talk to Rex and have him make it all go away.

CHAPTER FIVE

Mitzi got into her bright red Jaguar, a gift from Mitzi to herself, and began driving to Rex's home on the other side of town. When she was halfway there, she remembered he'd told her when they talked earlier in the day that he had a late consultation with a new patient who was flying in on her private plane from western Kansas. He'd laughed and said that if she had enough money to have a private plane and a pilot, he probably better be available for her. He told Mitzi to start thinking about where she wanted to go on their honeymoon, because this patient might very well provide the medical fees they needed to be able to pay for it.

Realizing Rex wouldn't be home, she turned around and drove to her house. Like everything else in Mitzi's life, it, too, had been affected when she'd gone through her mid-life crisis, or as she preferred to call it, change. The two story red brick house now had a bright red door, courtesy of a seminar she'd taken on feng shui. It was supposed to bring good luck, and based on Rex and everything else that had happened to her, she felt it had, at least until today.

Brightly painted white shutters flanked the French windows. Vibrant spring bedding plants lined the curved brick walkway leading to the house providing a multitude of colors which were repeated in the plants spilling out of large oak barrels on either side of the front door. Green grass accentuated the focal point of the front yard, a large graceful cottonwood tree, the state tree of Kansas.

She opened the garage door and drove in. Her cleaning lady had been there earlier in the day, and when Mitzi entered the house it gleamed with freshly oiled furniture and highly polished hardwood floors. She took a deep breath and felt better for the first time since she'd left her office at 4:30 to meet with Dr. Warren.

I will not go to the store and get a quart of ice cream and eat it, because it will make me sick, she repeated to herself several times. *What I will get is a glass of the chardonnay Rex brought over last night for dinner, and we didn't finish. One glass of that is probably a whole lot better for me than a quart of ice cream.*

After she poured herself a glass of wine, she went upstairs and walked down the hall to her large bedroom. When she began her mid-life change she decided she deserved to have a large bedroom with an adjoining sitting room. She had the wall separating the master bedroom from the small bedroom next to it taken out, and then she converted the smaller bedroom into a sitting room that had a couch and a flat screen television in it. Bookcases filled to full capacity lined the walls

Mitzi had opted for bright warm colors to get away from her past drabness, so the bedroom and the sitting room had been professionally decorated in shades of yellow and burnt orange accentuated with decorative items in white and turquoise. She'd come to think of it as her haven, her refuge from the world, and given the last hour, all she wanted to do was sit quietly in her refuge and figure out what she should do next.

She was sure Dr. Nguyen was the one who had written the anonymous note. Other than him, she couldn't think of anyone who would even remotely qualify as an enemy of hers. The problem was she had no idea how to combat the effect the note might have on Dr. Warren. Even if he didn't believe it, there would always be a shadow of doubt hanging over her that might make him think there was some truth to it.

Her phone rang, and she looked at the monitor. It was Dr. Warren. *Swell. I have no desire to talk to him, and if I did, I might say something I'd regret.* She let the call go to her voicemail, and after a few minutes she listened to the message he'd left on it.

"Dr. Green, I apologize for what happened this afternoon. I hope you know I wasn't accusing you of anything, I was simply trying to get to the bottom of a troubling situation. Obviously, it didn't go well. I want you to know I won't be making a decision regarding the assistant dean position for a few days. I've decided to not let the note enter into my decision or have any effect on it. Again, I'm sorry if I caused you pain. I'm quite aware I didn't handle it well. Have a pleasant evening."

Right, have a pleasant evening, she thought, throwing her shoe into the closet where it thudded against the back wall. It wasn't much, but the resounding thud made her feel better. Again, her phone rang. This time it was her fiancé.

"Oh, Rex, I'm so glad you called. I've just had the most horrible thing happen."

"Mitzi, are you all right?"

"Yes, I'm fine, but my professional reputation may not be."

"What are you talking about? You're one of the best, if not the best, acupuncturist this town has ever seen. I hear it all the time from patients of mine."

"Thanks, I needed that, but let me tell you what happened." She spent the next ten minutes filling him in on her conversation with Dr. Warren.

"Oh, honey, that is just so wrong. What a cowardly thing to do. I can't believe Dr. Nguyen would do something like that."

"I can. You've met him. Tell me you don't think he could do that."

Rex was quiet for a few moments and then said, "Yes, as arrogant and as filled with himself as he is, he could have done something like that, but surely someone would have seen him.”

“You'd think so,” Mitzi answered. “The problem is now I don't know what to do. Remember that book, Don Quixote, and how he tilted at windmills, his imaginary enemies? I feel that's what I'm doing. I have no idea who the enemy is, other than Dr. Nguyen. I know I'm starting to doubt myself, but what if it wasn't him? What if people do feel worse after I treat them?”

“Stop it, Mitzi. Quit feeling sorry for yourself. Someone at the university could be jealous of you, and it's not exactly a secret that you and Dr. Nguyen are both being considered for the position of assistant dean. The problem with the higher up you go, there's more people who are jealous you're at the top of the mountain, and they're not. For a lot of people, it's easier to throw stones than to try to make it to the top of that mountain.”

She was quiet for a moment, absorbing what he'd said. “You're probably right, Rex, but it doesn't feel very good. I have no idea what to do now, and I certainly don't know what I can do to refute something like this baseless allegation that's been made against me.”

“I don't think there's anything you can do about the note, but I have an off-the-wall idea. What if you circulated a petition among your patients and your students asking that you be named as the assistant dean? Dr. Warren would have to pay attention to something like that, and even if Binh got wind of it, if you sewed up the majority of the students, interns, and patients, he couldn't combat it. What do you think?”

“I think it's a fabulous idea, Rex. I've got all week to get the signatures. If I could get enough of them to sign it, I could present it to Dr. Warren late Friday afternoon. I'll get started on it when we finish talking.”

“Good. By the way, I also want to tell you how much I love you, and that I can't wait until we're married.”

"Oh, Rex, that's so sweet of you to say. I'm glad you feel that way, but that's not something I hear from you very often."

"No, and for that I apologize. I'll try to do better in the future. I guess what's behind it is a conversation I had with Dani, you know, my ex-fiancée. She still can't believe our relationship is over, and it was really an unpleasant conversation. She asked me what I saw in you that she didn't have. I told her I really couldn't answer that, I had just fallen totally in love with you and wanted to spend the rest of my life with you. I never realized what a small, mean-spirited woman she is."

"Rex, I have a feeling from the anger in your voice there was more to it than that. If you remember, we talked once about how important honesty is in a marriage. Don't think you're being totally honest with me at the moment. What else did she have to say?"

Rex took a deep breath and said, "She made some references to your past physical appearance. Evidently she'd looked you up on the Internet and found some old photos of you taken at some library appreciation dinner. She said once we were married, you'd revert back to your old appearance. She said all fat people did that. She told me she'd called the library and talked to someone who knew you when you worked there and learned they called you 'Fat Mitzi' behind your back. I'm sorry, honey, but you asked me to be candid."

"Rex, I'd be less than honest if I didn't tell you how much it hurts when I hear things like that, but I have to stay in the present, and presently, I am not fat, nor will I ever be again. Did your ex have anything else to say about me or our relationship?"

"Yes, she said she wished something bad would happen to you, so she and I could get married."

"How did you respond to that?"

"I told her that since nothing bad was going to happen to you, her wish was irrelevant. I also emphatically told her that she and I were never going to get married, and she better accept it."

"Thanks. Okay, enough of Dani. Let's go on to something else. How was your late patient today?"

"Very interesting, and she definitely will pay for our honeymoon. The woman was severely burned in a fire that broke out while she was in the barn at her cattle ranch. Evidently there were a bunch of oily rags in there that had been used for cleaning and then stored in a glass container. Unfortunately, whoever put them there didn't realize that linseed oil had been used in the cleaning process. They were tightly packed, which is a definite no-no."

"Why is that a no-no?" Mitzi asked.

"Because if they're in the sun, they get hot, and then you have a case of what's called spontaneous combustion, which is when a fire starts on its own without any obvious source of ignition like a match. The sun came in through a window in the loft. The glass intensified the sun's heat, and it was a perfect storm. A fire broke out, and my patient couldn't get out in time.

"Not only is she badly burned, but she fell from the loft and needs immediate surgery on her hip and her leg. Rather than have her undergo a number of operations, I need to call some orthopedic doctors tonight and schedule surgery for her as soon as possible. I'm going to be doing a large skin graft on her. She'll be fine when it's over, but it's a very painful procedure. When she called, she didn't tell me how badly she was injured. She had her nurse with her, and she was in a wheelchair.

"After her surgery, she's going to recuperate at the house I keep for post-surgery patients. It's the one you stayed at for a couple of days after your surgery. As you know, it's near my office, and the other doctors and I will be able to closely monitor her recovery. Anyway, that's a long roundabout way to tell you I won't be able to come over tonight. This is one of the few times since meeting you that business supersedes pleasure. Trust me, I'd much rather be with you, but I need to do this. I hope you understand."

"Of course, Rex. I'm just glad she had the foresight to call you.

Let me know what happens. I think I'll get started on my petition, and Rex, thanks for listening to me. I guess I was a little frantic when we started this conversation, but I feel much better now."

"Mitzi, one of the reasons I love you is because of the fine human being you are. Don't ever doubt yourself again." He paused for a moment and then laughed, "Of course, the package isn't too bad either."

"Good-bye Rex, go make someone beautiful. Love you!"

CHAPTER SIX

When Kat returned home after her lunch with Mitzi, Jazz, her white West Highland terrier, and Rudy, the big Rottweiler Blaine had bought for her when she was investigating Nancy's death, were both eagerly waiting by the door to the garage to greet her.

"Hi guys! Think it's time you both spent a little time outdoors. I've been gone a couple of hours, and I'm sure you can find things to do out there," she said as she let them out the back door. Rudy was a big dog and several months earlier he'd inadvertently walked through the screen door that led to the back yard. The side and bottom had torn loose from the screen door, and even though it wasn't particularly aesthetically appealing, it worked quite well as a doggie door during the warm spring days when Kat liked to keep the sliding glass door open. She looked at it for a moment, debating whether she should get it fixed before the wedding.

I have a feeling I'm going to be looking at everything through the eyes of the upcoming wedding. There are probably all kinds of things I need to do that I've ignored. Next time I talk to Lacie, I'll ask her. Daughters can sometimes be critical of their mothers, but I have to admit, she has a good eye.

Kat walked upstairs, changed clothes, and sat down at her computer. A few minutes later she was joined by Jazz and Rudy, who laid down on the dog beds she'd put in her office for them. She spent the next three hours on the Internet researching everything she could about acupuncturists, second chances, mid-life crises, and home weddings.

Kat even found one article that said baby boomers who rejected conventional marriages in their youth now wanted to reinvent old age by being a partner in a conventional marriage. This was one of the reasons cited for the upsurge in mid-life marriages it said. She knew Mitzi didn't technically qualify as a baby boomer, but maybe Rex did. In any event, she was glad her friend had found happiness and had made some mid-life changes that seemed to be working for her.

Thinking of Barbara and what she had said regarding Kat writing a book about Mitzi, she opened a new file on her computer and began to type in some ideas. The more she thought about it, the more interested she became in writing it. The one thing that bothered her was that there didn't seem to be much meat in the proposed book. Woman goes through mid-life crisis and becomes an acupuncturist. Woman loses weight. Woman becomes beautiful. Woman meets doctor, falls in love, and lives happily ever after.

She liked it so far, but it needed to have some tension built into it. Maybe she could have one of the doctor's ex-girlfriend's create problems. It was just too gooey sweet the way it was. Kat decided she'd start writing it in the morning. If it was anything like the other books she'd written, after a while the book would take on a life of its own, and it would dictate what was going to happen. It was as if Kat was reading the book while she was writing it.

Lost in reverie, it took a moment for her to realize her cell phone was ringing. She picked it up, looked at the monitor, and said, "Lacie, darling, how are you? How did the exam go this morning?"

"I think I did fine. I only have two more to go, and then I'm on summer break, well, not exactly because I'm going to summer school, but it will be nice to have this semester out of the way. What's new with you, Mom?"

Kat told her about Mitzi and the upcoming wedding. "Lacie, since the wedding and the reception are going to be here at the house, I'm wondering if you think I need to do anything to get it looking really good for the big event."

Lacie was quiet for a moment and then said, "Mom, are you sure this won't hurt your feelings?"

"What do you mean?" Kat asked.

"Well, it's kind of something I've noticed in a lot of my friend's parents' homes. They don't realize that some of the things in the house have become dated, because they live with them every day."

"I'm assuming you have something specific in mind."

"Yes. The door handles all look like they've been there ever since the house was built, which was before I was even born. I think it would make a world of difference if you updated those."

Kat was silent for a moment and then said with a sigh of resignation, "You're probably right. I'd just never thought about it. Is there anything else you can think of?"

"Mom, don't get mad at me, but I think you need to update the bathrooms and the kitchen with some new fixtures and appliances. It would be pretty easy to do, and since you only have a couple of months, there isn't time for a complete construction type of remodel."

"I'm not getting mad, Lacie, but I'd like to ask you a question. Do you think I need to completely redo the bathrooms and the kitchen?"

There was a pause before Lacie answered. "Mom, I think new fixtures and appliances would be all you'd need. That, along with new doorknobs, and you'd have the house looking spectacular. You could also pick up some fresh plants, maybe some of those orchids you love, and a couple of pillows for the couches and chairs, you know, accent kinds of things," she said as her voice speeded up. "It's going to just be great. I'd like to go with you when you shop for them. This is going to be fun."

"Lacie, I think you need to change your major from psychology to pre-law. You're very convincing, but then again, maybe that's part of psychology too. Get your exams out of the way, and then we'll do some shopping. Okay?"

"Okay. I may have some more ideas by then."

"Somehow I never doubted that, darling. Talk to you in a day or so. Study hard. Love you."

"Love you too, Mom."

CHAPTER SEVEN

Kat had just ended her call with Lacie when her phone rang again. This time it was Blaine, the newly elected district attorney she'd begun a relationship with several months earlier.

"How is Sexy Cissy this beautiful spring evening?" he asked using the pen name she used when she wrote her steamy romance novels.

"Very well, thank you. Actually Sexy Cissy is thinking about having Kat Denham write a cozy mystery. I've spent several hours researching it and making notes."

"I've never even heard that term. What's a cozy mystery?"

"Well, from what I understand the basic premise is that someone gets murdered and the main character, usually a woman who's an amateur sleuth, solves the murder. Often she has a relative, husband, or boyfriend who has something to do with law enforcement, so she can use his contacts when she needs help solving the case. Cozy mysteries generally don't have gore, overt sex, or swearing in them. They're usually not very long, and they tend to be in a series, because the readers become involved with the characters and want them to continue from one adventure to another."

"Interesting. Maybe I'm missing something, but why would you want to fool around with success? You've got a huge following, and your books are very popular. Why do you feel you need to try something new?"

"Truthfully, I'm getting a little bored. Let's face it, there are only so many ways you can write a steamy novel without getting into some areas I'm a little reluctant to research."

"Tell you what. Why don't I help with the research? Sounds like a good time to me," he said laughing.

"Blaine, I'm going to pretend I didn't hear that last remark and attempt to keep this relationship on a platonic basis, or at least a semi-platonic relationship."

His voice became serious, and he said, "Kat, I'd really like to make our relationship into something more than a get together for dinner and sharing a goodnight kiss and a hug. I think that's gone on long enough. I'd like to commit to a relationship with you, and I'd like it to be mutual. What do you say?"

"Blaine, you know how much I care for you, but I still need a little more time."

"Sweetheart, at our age the one thing we don't have the luxury of knowing is how much time we have left."

"You're probably right. What do you have in mind?"

She listened for a minute and said, "So you really would like me to consider having you move in here with me? Is that what you're saying? What would your straight-laced constituency think?"

His somewhat crude and descriptive answer made her laugh. "Blaine, you're getting very close to convincing me. Give me just a couple more days. If I said yes, what time frame are you looking at?"

Again she listened. "No, yesterday does not work for me. If I agreed, I think we'd need a few weeks to work out the details and yes, I'm very close to agreeing to it, if that's any consolation."

"Having never been married before, it scares me to even think about living with a woman, but Kat, I really would like to live with you."

"I don't recall hearing anything about marriage being included in your proposal," she said.

"Well, I probably haven't mentioned it, but maybe it's time. When you're taking all of this under consideration, consider that as well. Now I want to hear about your day."

She told him about her lunch with Mitzi and how she'd agreed to have the wedding and the reception at her home. "I understand you've played golf with Rex, her fiancé. What do you think of him?"

"He's a great guy. She couldn't do better. I'm kind of surprised to hear he's getting married, because he's completely devoted to his medical practice, probably too much. I know he was engaged to someone, but I wasn't at all surprised to hear he'd broken that off. When is the wedding going to take place?"

"In late July. I have about eight weeks to get everything ready. Lacie's going to help me update the house. We're going shopping for some new fixtures and appliances as well as some decorative items when she finishes her final exams."

"I'd like to go shopping with you, Kat. Since I'm going to be moving in, I think I should have some say in what you get, plus I'd like to help with the cost."

"You're really serious about this, aren't you, Blaine?"

"More than serious. I'd call it determined. So what color of appliances are we going to get? Actually, I think this is perfect timing. Right after they get married and at the reception, we can announce our upcoming marriage. What do you think?"

"You're assuming I'd say yes if you formally asked me, so what I think is the same thing I said a few minutes ago. I need a little more time to think about it."

"All right, I can live with that, although I want you to understand I'm saying that grudgingly. Sorry to have to end the call, but I need to prepare for a court case I have tomorrow. What's on your agenda for tomorrow?" he asked.

"Not much. I'm pretty serious about writing the book I mentioned earlier. I'd like to see if I can write successfully in another genre. I have a 10:00 appointment in the morning with Mitzi for my bi-weekly acupuncture treatment. After that I'll probably come home and write the rest of the day."

"Seriously, Kat? You're still going to her for that needle treatment stuff? Gives me the willies to even think about someone sticking needles in me. I really don't understand why anyone would consent to having someone jab needles in them. Sounds kind of masochistic to me."

"Blaine, it's a very ancient form of Eastern healing. The needles are inserted in several points called acupuncture points on a meridian for whatever ailment you have. My back is my problem. I'm sure I've developed arthritis, and I probably aggravate it by spending so much time sitting in front of my computer. I always feel better after a treatment, and I don't even feel the needles. Matter of fact, I don't even see them because I lie down on my front, and Mitzi inserts the needles in my back, above and below my waist. She applies a little electrical stimulus to four of the needles to activate the chi, that stands for energy in oriental medicine, and promote the healing. You may not think much of it, but acupuncture has really become a mainstream form of medical treatment in the last few years."

"I think you told me Mitzi teaches at the university, so it must have come into the mainstream if it's taught at a small university here in Kansas."

"It has, plus Mitzi told me she's being considered for the position of assistant dean of the department. That would be a pretty big deal."

"Does she have any competition, because that really does sound like a pretty big deal."

"From what she told me there's another doctor who also teaches at the university who's being considered. She not crazy about him."

"That's not unusual," Blaine said. "Whenever the stakes are high there's usually some friction between the ones being considered. Any idea when she'll find out if she got the job?"

"No. I'll ask her when I see her tomorrow. You better go prepare for your case. I don't want to be the reason you're not fully prepared," she said laughing.

"I will, but first I want to tell you that I love you. I know I've never said it before, but when you're considering our future, I'd like you to know I'm truly and hopelessly in love with you."

Kat's mouth seemed to outpace her brain, because she responded, "I love you, too." As soon as she said it she looked at her phone in amazement, not believing what she'd just said.

Blaine was quiet for a moment and then said, "You've just made me the happiest man in the world. You may not be ready to fully share your love, but I already know it's going to happen sometime very soon. Sweet dreams."

After she ended the call Kat sat for several moments in silence. Finally, she stood up and walked over to the back door, calling the dogs to come in. She knew her heart had said what her brain hadn't been able to and because of that, her world would never again be the same.

CHAPTER EIGHT

Kat opened the door to the acupuncture clinic at the university and walked over to the reception desk. "Hi, Rochelle, I have a 10:00 appointment this morning with Dr. Green."

"Of course, Mrs. Denham. Please follow me, and I'll show you which treatment room you'll be in." She opened the door and said, "This is my favorite room. It seems more cheerful and airy because of the window, even though we keep it closed. Dr. Green will be with you shortly."

Kat unsnapped and unzipped her jeans, knowing Mitzi would have to pull them down as well a push her blouse up in order to apply an acupuncture treatment to her low back area. She sat for a few minutes thinking about the book she was going to start when she got home.

There was a knock on the door, and Mitzi walked in wearing a doctor's white coat. "Kat, good to see you again. I thoroughly enjoyed lunch yesterday, but I have to say the rest of the day went downhill. Please lie down on the treatment table and get comfortable, and I'll get started."

While Mitzi inserted a number of small fine needles in her low back Kat asked, "What happened after you left? By the way, Lacie and Blaine both have thoughts on how I can spruce up the house in preparation for the wedding. It's going to make me get around to doing some things I've been putting off. Now tell me about yesterday."

Mitzi told her about her conversations with Rochelle, Dr. Warren, and finally Rex. When she'd concluded, she said, "I am so glad yesterday is over. I can't imagine having a worse day."

"Any idea when Dr. Warren is going to make his decision?" Kat asked.

"No, but last night I decided I don't care what happens, and that my marriage to Rex is far more important. If Dr. Nguyen is named as assistant dean, maybe it's for the best. I really want to make this marriage work, and I'm thoroughly committed to it. Kat, I just attached electrodes to four of the needles. I'll touch you where you should feel it, and when you feel a slight electrical tingle, let me know."

A few minutes later they heard Rochelle say, "Good morning, Mrs. Hendrick. Please follow me. You can go in this treatment room. Dr. Green will be with you shortly."

"Everything okay, Kat?" Mitzi asked.

"Yes, I'm fine, I can feel a little tingling where you attached the electrodes."

"Okay. I need to get Mrs. Hendrick set up. I'll be back and check on you in a few minutes. Just relax." She turned off the overhead light as she walked out and left the door slightly ajar.

Several minutes went by and Kat continued to feel the slight electrical impulse from the electrodes attached to the needles. She spent the time planning her book, but was frustrated by what she felt was the lack of any exciting action in the story.

Well, since the whole thing is a figment of my imagination anyway, I'll just have to create some sort of exciting action. Once I start writing, it will probably come to me.

There was a knock on the door to her room, and Kat heard Dr. Green say, "Everything okay?"

"Yes, I'm fine," Kat answered.

"Good, you only have ten minutes more. I'll be back when the machine chimes to let me know your treatment is finished."

After what must have been ten minutes, the chimes went off, and the gentle electric pulsation in her lower back stopped. A moment later Dr. Green came into the room. "That will do it for today, Kat. I'll give you a call in a day or so, and we can start making plans for the wedding. I'm going to be talking to a caterer and a florist, but I'd like your input before I meet with either of them. Is that okay with you?"

"Fine, Mitzi. See you then." Kat fastened her jeans and walked out to the reception desk. "Okay, Rochelle, how much do I owe?"

"It will be $65.00. How do you want to pay?"

"Please put it on my Visa. Let me get it out of my purse." As Kat was unzipping her purse she heard Mitzi shout in a loud voice, "Rochelle, quick, call 911. Tell them there's a medical emergency and to get here immediately."

Kat hurried down the hall to where Mitzi's voice had come from and walked into one of the treatment rooms. Mitzi was standing next to a woman who was lying on her back on a treatment table. Her eyes were closed, and from what Kat observed, she wasn't breathing.

"Mitzi, what's wrong?" Kat asked, putting her hand on Mitzi's shoulder which was shaking. "What's happened?"

"I have no idea. I walked into the room when there was about ten more minutes left for her treatment and asked Sandy if she was all right. She didn't answer, so I turned on the light. I looked at her and asked her again. She never answered because she's dead. I can't believe this. I knew she had high blood pressure, but every time she's come here her blood pressure has been much lower after a treatment. I check it before and after."

Soon they both heard a siren and within minutes the room was filled with firemen and emergency medical technicians. They took Sandy Hendrick's vital signs and tried to restart her heart. Their efforts were in vain. She was dead. After several minutes, one of the paramedics covered her body with a sheet and said, "I need to call the county coroner. The body can't be moved until he officially pronounces her dead, and I've already notified the police. Even though it looks like she probably had a heart attack, it's part of our standard operating procedure which we're required to follow. Her next of kin also needs to be notified."

Mitzi stammered, "I'll get her file and take care of notifying her husband. I know it's a second marriage, and she doesn't have any children. I don't know what happened. She was fine when she came in."

With tears rolling down her cheeks, Mitzi walked out of the room accompanied by Kat. By the time they'd walked to the front desk, several policemen had arrived and were walking back to the treatment room where Sandy Hendrick's body was.

"Who's in charge here?" a portly mustached policemen asked.

"I'm Dr. Green," Mitzi said. "What do you need from me?"

The policeman said, "I'm Detective Shafer. I'll be investigating the woman's death. I need to take a statement from you and your receptionist. Was anyone else here when you discovered her?"

"My receptionist, Rochelle was here. The only other person that was here in the clinic this morning is Mrs. Denham," Mitzi said, nodding in Kat's direction.

"Mrs. Denham, you need to stay here until I've had an

opportunity to talk to you. I don't know yet if this is a murder case, but I'm not going to take any chances. Although it doesn't look like it, there's always a chance it was. Each of you is considered to be a suspect until we find out how the decedent died. Dr. Green, do you have an office I can use?"

"Yes. I need to call the decedent's husband first, if you don't mind."

"Dr. Green, I'll take care of that for you," Rochelle said. "I'll just tell her husband I'm calling on your behalf."

Mitzi motioned for the detective to follow her down the hall to her office. He turned to Kat and said, "I don't know how long this will take, but if you have something else scheduled, you might want to cancel it. From what I hear there aren't any signs of foul play, but sometimes that doesn't mean much."

For some reason, Kat happened to be looking at Rochelle when the policemen spoke to her, and when she thought about it later, she would swear that just for a moment, a fleeting smile had crossed Rochelle's face. It happened so quickly she wondered if she'd imagined it.

CHAPTER NINE

An hour and a half later, after the coroner and his assistant had taken Sandy Hendrick's body to the county morgue, and the police and firemen had left, Kat felt she could leave as well.

"Mitzi, I'm going to leave now. Why don't you do the same? Have Rochelle call your patients and cancel the rest of your appointments for today. I'm sure you could use some quiet time after the events of this morning."

"I wish I could, Kat, but as backed up as my appointments are now because of this, I really need to get busy. People come to me to be healed, and I can't let them down." She turned to Rochelle. "I haven't had a chance to ask you, but were you able to get in touch with Sandy's husband?"

"Yes. I called him at the work number that was in her file. Naturally he was shocked. He thanked me for calling and said he was certain it had something to do with her high blood pressure."

"As tragic as this is," Mitzi said, "I hope the same thing. Certainly there weren't any signs of foul play, but having someone die when they're in your care is not a pleasant experience. I'll bet Dr. Nguyen will spread it all over as soon as he hears about it, if he hasn't already."

"Did the coroner say when he'd have the autopsy report?" Kat asked.

"He said he was going to conduct the autopsy this afternoon. Evidently it takes several hours. He also mentioned the report itself probably wouldn't be available for at least a week, and if they found something unusual, maybe longer. That's one full week my reputation is bound to suffer. I'm sure some people will think I had something to do with it," Mitzi said.

"You know, Blaine, the man I've been seeing a lot of lately, is the district attorney. I'll bet he knows the coroner. Maybe he can get the process speeded up. I'll call him when I get home. Is there anything else I can do for you before I leave?"

"No, Kat, thanks for offering. I'm sorry you were involved, but I have to say I'm glad you were here. You kept me from falling apart. I'll call you tonight. I need to let all of this sink in. Thanks again."

Kat walked to her car, feeling very unsettled. It was bad enough to have someone die in the treatment room next to hers, but there was a thought that hadn't been voiced by either Kat or Mitzi. What if Sandy Hendrick's death wasn't caused by her high blood pressure? If that was the case, she wondered if Mitzi would be a suspect, or even if she herself would be. The detective had hinted as much. She definitely needed to talk to Blaine.

As soon as she got home she opened the back door to let Jazz and Rudy out. The makeshift doggie screen door could work for the rest of the afternoon. She walked down the hall, went into her office, and took her phone out of her purse. A moment later she heard Blaine's voicemail. She asked him to call her when he had a minute, remembering he'd told her last night he'd be in court today.

She sat down at her computer, checked her messages, and then brought up the Word document she'd started and saved yesterday afternoon. She saw the working title for the book she'd been thinking about, "Murder and Acupuncture." She looked down at the screen and couldn't believe what she'd typed yesterday. It was as if her fingers must have had a life of their own when they typed it. She didn't consciously remember her brain linking to her fingers and typing the words she saw displayed on the screen before her.

While she was staring at the screen, her phone rang and she saw Blaine's name appear on the screen. "I am so glad you called," she began. He quickly interrupted her.

"Kat, are you all right?" he asked worriedly.

"Yes, why do you ask?"

"I just got a call from the county coroner. He notifies me whenever there's been a death, so I'll be in the loop in case it turns out criminal activity was involved. When he notified me a death had occurred at the acupuncture clinic at the university, all I could think of was you told me you had an appointment there this morning. I panicked. Poor guy. I remember practically yelling into the phone, 'What's the name of the decedent?' When he told me, and I realized it wasn't you, it took me a couple of minutes to regain enough composure to explain to him why I wanted to know."

"Oh, Blaine, that's sweet."

"No, it's not sweet. It made me realize more than ever that I want you to be my wife. That just sealed it. Kat, will you marry me?"

She was quiet for several moments and then she said, "Although this has to be about the strangest circumstance surrounding a marriage proposal anyone's probably ever had, the answer is yes, Blaine, yes."

"Tell you what," he said. "Let's get married this fall at the country club. I'll do the old-fashioned thing and not move in until after we're married. As soon as I finish with this case, I'll get a proper engagement ring for you. Any preferences?"

"No. This whole conversation is surreal. I just said yes to marrying a man on the phone. He's in court, and I spent all morning with a dead woman. This sounds like something out of a novel. Actually, I may put it in a novel."

"I'll come by tonight after I get out of court, and we can work out some of the details for our wedding. You know I've never been married before. Do you think I should wear white?" he asked laughing.

"Since nothing else about this whole conversation has been traditional, why not have the groom wear white? Blaine, I need you to be serious for a few minutes."

"You're right. I was probably out of line with that last comment, but trust me, I've never been more serious about anything in my life when it comes to making you my wife."

"No, you weren't out of line at all. The coroner said he was going to conduct the autopsy on the dead woman, Sandy Hendrick, this afternoon. I know that tests often need to be done to positively confirm something, and it may take weeks, but isn't there some way to get a preliminary report earlier than that? The reason I'm asking is even though there's no reason for it, there's bound to be a dark cloud hanging over Mitzi's reputation until the death is determined to have been caused by natural causes. I can't believe this will be good for her acupuncture practice, particularly given the fact she's being considered for the job of assistant dean."

"I've known Greg Santos for a long time. That's the coroner's name. As a matter of fact, we usually play golf on Saturdays at the club during the summer. I'll give him a call and see if he can give me an expedited report, or even release one to the press saying the death was due to natural causes. However, there is something you need to think about, Kat."

"What's that?"

"What are you going to do if the death wasn't due to natural causes? What if the woman was murdered? I know it sounds bizarre, but stranger things have happened, believe me."

"Blaine, I believe you, but I was there. Everyone from the coroner to the police agreed there was no sign of foul play. I was in that room with the dead woman. If she was murdered, I can't imagine how it could have happened."

"I hope for your friend Mitzi's sake, that's true. If not, it could cause big problems for her, and you might even be under suspicion since you were there when the woman died."

"You're kidding, right? Why would I be implicated? I didn't even know the woman."

"When a murder occurs, everyone who was physically present, who knew the victim, or who had anything to do with the victim, is looked at as a possible suspect. I'm sure this is unnecessary, but I'm going to call Nick and put him on alert that we may need his services."

"Blaine, I think you're overreacting. I know your brother Nick's a great private investigator, and he sure helped me when my editor was murdered, but this seems a little over the top."

"Be that as it may, I'm going to do it. I'll call Greg and Nick now, and I'll see you later. And Kat, thanks."

"For what? I didn't do anything."

"You agreed to marry me. I think that's doing something."

"No, I'm the one that should be saying thank you for asking. See you tonight."

CHAPTER TEN

Promptly at six that evening the doorbell rang. Kat was in the kitchen fixing dinner when she heard the joyful yelps of the dogs. That, along with the doorbell, announced Blaine's arrival.

She opened the door and hugged the man who would soon be her husband. Pulling away, she looked at him and thought, *along with being one of the finest people she'd ever met, he really is attractive with the grey hair at his temples highlighting his tanned face.* Blaine was known to sneak out to the golf course whenever the weather was good, and he felt he could get away from the office. The only thing that gave him away was his tan. No one who knew him would even think of suggesting that the tan came from a sunlamp. No, Blaine was the kind of man whose tan came from being outdoors, and in his case, that was the golf course.

Blaine looked down at her and smiled, pulling her to him once again and kissing her deeply. She gently pushed him away and led him into the house. "That should give the neighbors something to talk about," she said laughing.

"Since the word is already out you're Sexy Cissy, I don't think it will come as a shock to anyone that you engage in behavior like that. I'm going to let the dogs out for a moment. Mind if I close the back door, so they can't get in?"

"Of course not, but why so serious?"

He walked over and told the dogs to go outside and then closed the door. When he returned he got down on one knee in front of her and said, "Kat Denham, will you marry me?"

"Blaine, I told you I would over the phone. Please, get up. You don't have to do this."

"No. I want to do this by the book, and from everything I've heard, this is how proposals are supposed to be done. Now, answer the question."

"Yes! The answer is yes. Now will you please stand up?"

He stood up, kissed her, and then took a small box out of his pocket. "Kat, if you want another ring, I'll completely understand. I think I told you a while ago that my family was very wealthy. This is my grandmother's ring, and I inherited it when she died. I've never done anything with it, and if you like the stone, I'd like to have a more modern setting designed for you. If you don't like the stone, we'll find something you do like."

She opened the small box, looked at it, looked up at him, and then looked again at the ring. "Blaine this is the most beautiful ring I've ever seen," she said with tears in her eyes. "It's far too expensive for me to wear. It's absolutely spectacular. I've never seen anything like it."

"You probably haven't. From the family stories I was told, it's extremely rare," he said.

"What's the stone? It's really different."

"It's called a fancy purplish pink heart shaped diamond. I guess the cut, the color, and the fact that it's two carats makes it pretty rare. The setting is old-fashioned, but if you like the diamond, as I said, I'll have a new setting designed for you."

"No. Absolutely not. I've never had anything like this in my life, and I think the setting is beautiful. If you're serious about giving me this, I would consider it an honor to wear your grandmother's ring."

"Well, in that case, let's see if it fits." He put the ring on her finger and gently kissed her. "Kat, it's as if it was made for you."

She moved her ring finger around while the late afternoon sun pouring in from the living room window played off of the large diamond, creating a kaleidoscope of rainbow colors throughout the room.

"Blaine, I think we need to celebrate this. I have a very good bottle of champagne in the refrigerator I was going to offer Lacie when she finished her exams this semester, but I think this occasion warrants it instead. I'll get another one for her. Would you open it? I need to check on a couple of things for dinner."

"Kat, you can celebrate this with champagne if you like, and I'll help you, then later I'd like to celebrate it my way, and you can help with that," he said grinning.

"We'll see."

"Yeah, I guess I should be used to it by now. Promises, promises, promises, but you can't blame a man for trying," he muttered audibly as he walked toward the kitchen.

Jazz and Rudy had been watching them intently through the sliding glass back door, wondering why Blaine had gotten down on one knee and then why they put their faces together. When Blaine walked toward them, they knew they'd probably be let in if they woofed, and so they did, and so they were.

Kat went into the kitchen and checked on the osso buco which was simmering on the range. While she was heating some olive oil and butter in a large pan for the risotto, Blaine walked over and handed her a filled champagne flute.

"Kat, can you put the spoon down for a minute? I'd like to propose a toast."

"Absolutely," she said, raising her glass.

"Here's to making me the happiest man in the world," he said as he gently touched his glass to hers.

"Well, I certainly don't want to be outdone. Here's to making me the happiest woman in the world, thank you." Again they touched their glasses and each took a sip. "That's really good. Wow! I could get used to this. Champagne for lunch yesterday and champagne tonight." Her words were interrupted by a sizzling sound coming from the kitchen stove. "Think I better take care of this, or I'm going to burn the beginnings of the risotto."

"What's in that big dish on the back burner, Kat? It smells wonderful."

"It's a dish called osso buco. I don't eat veal very often, but when I was at the store yesterday I saw some veal shanks and remembered how good the osso buco was when I had it years ago at an Italian restaurant. I'm going to serve it over risotto. Since asparagus is definitely in its prime in the spring, I decided to add some of that to it. Go watch the news. Dinner will be ready in about forty-five minutes."

He walked over to the television set in the great room and turned it on. A few minutes later she heard the talking head news commentator going on and on about all the disasters that had taken place in the world on that particular day. She shook her head in dismay at the carnage displayed on the screen. *What's the old saying about television news?* She thought. *I think its if it bleeds, it leads.*

*****

"Okay, Blaine, dinner is on the table. Wearing a ring this big is going to take a little getting used to, and I sure don't want to take it off and lose it. I have to keep pinching myself to believe all this is happening."

"Believe it," he said as he sat down at the table. "Kat, this looks fabulous. The meat on the veal shanks is literally falling off the bone."

"Hope it's as good as it looks."

They were both quiet for a few minutes while they ate, and then Blaine said, "It's definitely as good as it looks. I know you said earlier you don't eat much veal, but any time you're inclined to make this, you'd make me a very happy man."

"Good. Glad you like it. Blaine, when we talked on the phone today, you mentioned you were going to call your friend, the coroner. Did you, and if so, what did he say?"

"Sorry, with everything else, it slipped my mind. Yes, I did. He'd just gotten back from lunch, and he was getting ready to do the autopsy. He told me if he found anything out, he'd give me a call tonight. The fact he hasn't called is probably good news."

"Wait a minute. The guy did an autopsy after he ate lunch? Seriously?"

"Yeah, I know. I sure couldn't do that, but I guess after you do enough autopsies, it just becomes part of your routine."

"I don't think I could ever have an autopsy become routine."

"Agreed. Ah, sorry, but I hear my phone. It's in the pocket of my suit coat which I hung up in the hall closet. Mind if I go talk to whoever it is?"

"Of course not. I'll clean up while you're talking." She cleared the table and rinsed the dishes while Blaine took the call.

A few minutes later she heard him walk into the kitchen, and when she turned around, she noticed how serious he looked. "Is something wrong, Blaine?"

"Yes. Greg doesn't think the woman who died in Mitzi's office died from natural causes. He thinks she was poisoned."

"Oh, no," gasped Kat. "I've got to call Mitzi and tell her."

"Wait a minute. Kat, Greg told me if he discovers that foul play may have been involved in a death, he's required to call the chief of police and tell him before it's released to the public. He's making that call now. I imagine that both you and Mitzi will be visited by the police tonight or first thing tomorrow morning. Greg said they'd probably treat this as a murder case. The police will be interviewing anyone and everyone who knew her."

"Are you telling me Mitzi and I may become suspects in her murder? Is that what you're saying?"

"Yes, I'm afraid so. Now why don't you call Mitzi, and then I want you to tell me exactly what happened this morning. I want to know everything, who was there, what was said, everything. I alerted Nick earlier. I'm going to call him and have him come over, so he can get started immediately on any investigation stuff that needs to be done."

"As district attorney, can't you make this go away or do something? You know that neither Mitzi nor I murdered her."

"I wish I could, sweetheart, but I really don't have anything to do with a case until it's brought to me by the police, and their evidence is presented to me. Then I make a determination whether or not we should file a criminal complaint against someone. Believe me, when people find out the district attorney's fiancée is a suspect in a murder case, unfortunately that alone will cause it to make the papers."

"Oh, Blaine, I'm so sorry you have to be involved."

"Kat, we don't have much time. Call Mitzi, and then we need to get started on clearing both your names. I can't do anything publicly, but I can sure give you and Mitzi some thoughts on what you need to do."

She looked down at her ring, wondering if she'd done the right thing when she accepted it or if she was going to be a huge liability to Blaine.

CHAPTER ELEVEN

"Hi, Mitzi, it's Kat. I can't talk for very long, but I'm afraid I have some bad news. You know how I mentioned that Blaine's the district attorney. Well, it turns out the coroner is a friend of his. Blaine asked him if he'd let Blaine know the preliminary results from the autopsy before it was released to the public. The coroner just called Blaine and he's pretty sure your patient was poisoned. He's having tests run to confirm it. Blaine is sure you and I will be investigated and could even become suspects in the case. He said it will probably be investigated as a murder case."

"What? Oh, no!" Mitzi exclaimed with a sound of shock in her voice. "You've got to be kidding. This is about as bad as it gets. I can just hear what Dr. Nguyen will say about this. I might as well kiss that promotion goodbye. I better call Rex and tell him, before he hears it from someone else. Don't think he's going to be too happy his fiancée may be considered as a suspect. This is just swell. Kat, I've got to make some calls, and I'm sure you do too. Let's talk tomorrow."

*****

"In all honesty, Kat, this really is not how I envisioned we would spend our first night together as an engaged couple. There are a lot of other things I would prefer to do, but while you were talking to Mitzi I called Nick, and he's on his way over here right now. I think there's some saying about two heads being better than one, and in this case, I think three heads will even be better."

"Blaine, are you sure that was necessary? After all, Nick's one of the top private investigators in the state. Isn't bringing him in to look at the case unnecessary and a little premature?"

"No, the quicker we can establish who might be a suspect, besides you and Mitzi, the quicker Nick can get started on this. Of course it's important to find out how Sandy Hendrick was poisoned, but it's equally important to clear both your name and Mitzi's from the list of suspects. Good, there's the doorbell. Must be Nick. Why don't you get some pens and paper, and we'll get started as soon as he comes in?"

When Blaine walked back into the great room he was followed by a tall handsome man who definitely resembled Blaine. It didn't take much of a leap of imagination to know they must have come from the same gene pool. "Kat, it's good to see you again," Nick said as he kissed her cheek, "and I understand congratulations are in order, although it sounds like you may have to table those wedding plans until we get this little problem under control."

"Nick, I really wish we were seeing each other under different circumstances. Hopefully, after you become my brother-in-law, we'll be able to get together when someone's death isn't the main reason for meeting. Where should we start?"

"Blaine gave me the bare bones when he called this afternoon. I want to know everything that took place from the time you got to Dr. Green's office until the time you left."

Even though Kat told him what she thought was everything, several times Nick interrupted her with questions. "Kat, you said you checked in with a receptionist by the name of Rochelle. Do you know her last name?"

"I've only called her Rochelle since the time I've been going there for acupuncture treatments, but there's a nameplate on the reception counter, and I'm pretty sure her last name is Salazar."

"That's a good start. I need more details like a physical description, what she did before she started working for Dr. Green, things of that nature."

"She's about age forty-five, around 5'5" tall, with dark hair worn short framing her olive complexion. I think she has brown eyes. She's quite attractive. I remember Mitzi telling me that after her children left home, her husband left her. Even though she had a college degree, she'd never worked outside the home. Evidently she wanted to try something different, and she entered the acupuncture program at the university. I think maybe she's in her last year. It seems to me Mitzi mentioned once that she was going to have to find a new receptionist next year because Rochelle would be a licensed acupuncturist and wouldn't want to work as a receptionist any longer."

"Good. That's enough for me to get started. Do you know where she lives?" Nick asked.

"I have no idea. Would you like me to call Mitzi? She probably knows."

"Not yet. I may have some other questions I want to ask her, and I might as well do them all at once."

"How about the woman who died? What's her name?"

"Sandy Hendrick."

"Do you know anything about her? From what I understand you saw her even though she was deceased. Can you give me her physical description?"

"I'd say she looked to be in her mid-forties. She had shoulder length blond hair which was probably professionally highlighted. I never saw her eyes, because Mitzi had mercifully closed them."

"Do you know if she was married or had children?"

"Nick, I remember Mitzi telling the detective she needed to call Sandy's husband and tell him, but Rochelle volunteered to do it," she said becoming quiet for a few minutes as she thought back to the conversation, "because the detective wanted to question Mitzi. I also remember she was wearing a wedding ring. I think Mitzi said something about her not having any children."

"When we call Mitzi, I'll see if she knows his first name. That would help. So other than you, Rochelle, Mitzi, and Sandy Hendrick, no one else was in the acupuncture clinic." Kat nodded affirmatively. "What can you tell me about Mitzi?"

Kat told him about Mitzi's mid-life crisis or change as she called it, and how she was going to be married in two months to Dr. Rex Brown, a plastic surgeon. Blaine interrupted her and said, "Nick, I've known Rex for years. He's a really good man. If he's marrying Mitzi, she's above reproach."

"Blaine, you know everyone has to be looked at in this type of case."

"Are you saying Mitzi really could be a suspect?" Kat asked incredulously.

"I'm not saying anyone is a suspect. That's not my job. My job is to get facts and information about these people. There's a big difference."

"Yes, I see what you're saying, but there may be a couple of other people you might want to check out."

Nick looked up from the pad of paper he'd been writing on. "Go on, Kat, if there's anyone else you think I need to know about, don't hold back."

She told him about the conversation she'd had with Mitzi regarding Dr. Warren, Dr. Nguyen, and also Mitzi's conversation with Rex regarding his ex-fiancée saying she hoped Mitzi would have an accident.

"Do you know the name of the ex-fiancée?"

"No. I don't know if Mitzi even knows her name."

"Why don't you call Mitzi? I'd like to talk to her."

"Of course." She picked up her phone from the table and pressed in Mitzi's number. A moment later it was answered by Mitzi, who was sobbing. "Mitzi, it's Kat. What's wrong?"

CHAPTER TWELVE

"Oh Kat, it was horrrriiibbble," Mitzi sobbed.

"Mitzi, I don't know what you're talking about. Please, tell me what's going on."

"It was the police. They were just here along with that detective we talked to earlier today. They searched my house and my car. Can you believe it? I felt like a criminal, and then they took my computer, after I agreed to let them take it."

"Why would they take your computer?"

"They told me they wanted to see if there was anything on it that might relate to Sandy's death. Oh, Kat, I think they suspect me of killing Sandy. I don't know what I'm going to do," she wailed.

"Mitzi, calm down. I have someone here who is going to help us. It's Blaine's brother, and he's a private investigator. Blaine called him this afternoon when Blaine found out that it looked like the woman was poisoned. He told his brother to come over, so he could get started with an investigation right away. He needs to ask you some questions. Believe me, he was a huge help when I was involved in that murder case a couple of months ago. Trust me, he can help."

Mitzi stopped crying and said, "What does he need to know? I'm not sure I can help, but I'll try."

"I'm going to let you talk to him. His name's Nick." She handed the phone to Nick and covered it with her hand. "Nick, she's pretty emotional right now. The police were at her house searching it and questioning her. They took her computer."

"That's pretty standard. I rather imagine they'll be here for yours pretty soon as well." He took the phone from her. "Hi, Mitzi, this is Nick Evans. There are a few questions I'd like to ask you, so I can get started with this investigation. First of all, what can you tell me about Sandy Hendrick?"

Mitzi told him what she knew including the fact that her husband's name was Matt. She said she thought he was an engineer, but she didn't know where he worked.

"Can you tell me why Sandy came to you? What were you treating her for?" he asked.

There was silence on the other end of the phone, and then Mitzi said, "Nick, when I became a doctor I took an oath not to reveal what I was treating a patient for. There is a caveat to that. When the patient is deceased, in acupuncture, as opposed to some other forms of medicine, an acupuncture doctor is no longer bound by that oath. The police asked me the same question, and I told them I was treating her for depression, and that's the truth."

"Do you know if her depression was chronic or situational?" Nick asked.

"I know her marriage wasn't a happy one. It was a second marriage for both she and her husband, and she told me it was as if they were circling the drain, waiting to be sucked down it. She said this wasn't the first time she'd been depressed, as she'd suffered bouts of depression all her life. I'm not a psychologist and make no pretense of being one, but it was obvious to me Sandy was clinically depressed."

"Mitzi, I'm a little unclear how acupuncture can help something like depression. I kind of get it when it comes to helping cure physical ailments by unblocking things, as I understand it, but depression?"

"Actually, it's quite common for acupuncturists to treat people for depression. There are certain lines in the human body we call meridians. You'd probably call them channels. When they're blocked, or the chi, called the energy in oriental medicine, is blocked, they can cause depression in a person. When they become unblocked the physical sense of depression is gone, however, that doesn't mean that the underlying causes of the depression aren't still there."

"Okay, I see what you mean. Did she ever mention they were going to get divorced?"

"No, once she told me her husband kept telling her he didn't want a divorce, because he loved her. Another time she mentioned she suspected he was having an affair because she smelled perfume on him. I think she said it was Amerige. She recognized it, because it was the same one she liked to wear."

"Maybe I'm being thick here, but if she wore the same perfume couldn't she have smelled her own perfume on him?"

"I asked her the same question," Mitzi answered. "She told me it wasn't her perfume because for a long time they hadn't been intimate enough for her perfume to be on him."

"All right, I get the picture. Let me ask you a couple of other questions. Do you know where your receptionist, Rochelle Salazar, lives?"

"Yes. Let me walk into my study. I keep her personnel file at home in my desk. Here it is. She lives at 473 East Mesa Drive here in town. Does that help?"

"Very much. What can you tell me about Dr. Nguyen? I understand you both are being considered for an appointment to the same position."

"Yes we are, although I think I can kiss it off after this incident." She proceeded to tell Nick everything she knew about Dr. Nguyen. "That's about it. Anything else?"

"Yes, one more thing. I understand your fiancé, Dr. Brown, and you had a conversation yesterday relating to his ex-fiancée. What do you know about her?"

"Not much. I believe she's a paralegal, and that her name is Dina. I don't know who she works for or where she lives. I could ask Rex, but I'm a little reluctant to do that, although he was wonderful when I spoke with him a few minutes ago."

"I understand. Since Blaine's in the legal field, maybe he can find something out about her. I think that's all I need from you for now. I may have some more questions when I get a little deeper into this."

"Good," Mitzi said. "I have to teach tomorrow morning, and in the afternoon I'll be with my interns. If I can help, please call. I really am desperate to clear my name. Please do whatever you need to do."

"Dr. Green, I'm sure you understand I can't promise anything, but I'll do my best. I have a number of people working for me who can find out almost anything about someone. I'm going to go home now and get started on this. Get a good night's sleep."

"Thanks for your help, Nick. I feel a lot better than I did when this conversation started."

He put down the phone and turned to Blaine. "Since I had her on speakerphone, I'm sure you heard everything. I'd like you to see if you can find out who Dina, the paralegal, is. As I told Dr. Green, I want to get started on this right away. Kat, I'll call you tomorrow."

He was interrupted by the sound of the doorbell. Rudy ran to the front door and started growling. Jazz took refuge under the sofa. She was terrified when Rudy growled, knowing there had to be a reason for it, and it usually wasn't something good.

"Rudy, stay! Who is it?" Kat asked as she looked through the peephole. She heard the words, "It's the police," but as soon as she saw the uniforms she knew that the police who had been at Mitzi's house earlier were now standing on her doorstep. She recognized Detective Shafer as the man who had led the investigation in Mitzi's office.

"Let them in," Blaine said walking over to the door. He opened it, and for a moment there was an awkward silence as Detective Shafer tried to figure out what the district attorney was doing at the home of the woman he was going to interrogate in a possible murder case and could, in fact, be a suspect.

"Please come in. My fiancée and I were discussing our wedding plans with my brother. Actually we became engaged today, so there's a lot to talk about. How can we help you?" Blaine asked.

"Congratulations, sir. We're here to talk to Mrs. Denham," Detective Shafer said, having recovered from his surprise at seeing Blaine at Kat's home. "She was at an acupuncture clinic this morning when another patient died. Unfortunately, there's a good chance the woman didn't die from natural causes. We need to do an in-depth interview."

"Certainly. I see no reason why, as her husband-to-be, I can't sit in on the conversation, do you?"

"Of course not, sir. This shouldn't take too long," Detective Shafer said.

"I need to get home," Nick said. "Talk to you soon and congratulations to both of you." He shook Blaine's hand and kissed Kat on the cheek.

Detective Shafer recognized him, but given the fact that Kat was wearing a diamond on her finger that hadn't been there this morning, and Nick was the district attorney's brother, he decided to let it slide that Nick might be there for a reason other than celebrating the engagement.

"Let's go into the great room, Detective," Kat said. "There's a large table in there we can sit at, and I'll be happy to tell you what I know, although I think I told you everything this morning."

"You probably did, but I'd like you to try and recall if there is anything else. Did you hear something odd? Were there unexplained footsteps in the hall or doors opening?"

"I'm sorry, but as I said, I don't think I know any more now than I did then. What makes you think she didn't die from natural causes?" Kat asked.

The detective looked at Blaine and then back to Kat. It was apparent to both of them that the detective was wondering how much they knew about the coroner's report. He decided he'd better be honest, or there could be a problem in the future.

"The coroner issued a preliminary report stating he'd found a substance in her body which appeared to be a poison. Naturally, when information like that is discovered, we go back to square one. One of the reasons we took DNA evidence and dusted the treatment room for fingerprints this morning was because there's always a possibility the coroner's report will show something other than what was thought to be death from natural causes. That seems to be the case here."

"I find it hard to believe that a woman goes to an acupuncture treatment and then dies from a poison. Surely it must have been something she was exposed to or ingested earlier in the day," Kat said.

"One would think so, but then again you never know. Since you don't seem to have any more information, I think we'll be leaving. Oh," he said turning back to her, "I'd like permission to take your computer and have one of our experts look at it. In this age of technology, it's become a very important part of our investigations."

"Wait a minute," Blaine said with an edge in his raised voice, "Why do you want to see Kat's computer? What in the devil do you expect to find? A confession? Of course if she confesses to murder, I'll have to recuse myself from prosecuting her since she's my fiancée."

"I'm sure we'll be returning it by noon tomorrow. It's simply procedure, sir. You know how the court and police systems work. Everything has to be done properly and by the book."

"It's in my office down the hall, the second door on the left. You're welcome to take it," Kat said. "Detective, will all the information on it remain intact? The reason I ask is because I'm an author, and although I've backed up all my books on the Cloud, I'd be panicked if anything was lost, because I have everything regarding them on it."

"That depends on what we find. More than likely, someone will bring it back to you by noon tomorrow. I'm assuming there's nothing on it that would present a problem to you."

"Of course not."

"Okay, I'll be in touch if there's anything else I need. Time is of the essence in murder cases, so we're already working on it. Hopefully, it won't take long. Have a nice rest of your evening, although there isn't much left of it, and again, congratulations on your engagement," he said as he and the other policeman left.

CHAPTER THIRTEEN

"Kat, this has been a very long day for you," Blaine said once the policemen had left. "I'd love to stay for a while, but given everything that's happened today, I think I'll table the thought of celebrating our engagement for some other time. You need to get some sleep."

"Thanks for being so understanding. It's hard to take it all in. I've gotten engaged, and a woman died in the treatment room next to mine. While I haven't been named as a suspect, I'm getting the distinct impression that the detective thinks I may have had something to do with it."

"No, don't worry, they always act like that. Trust me. Once they see there's nothing on your computer that could be a problem for you, they'll forget about you. They're just following routine police procedure. Kat, what's wrong?" Blaine asked. "You've turned pale, and you look like you're going to faint."

Suddenly she collapsed onto a nearby couch and put her face in her hands, emitting a mournful "Oh, no."

"Kat, what is it? Please, tell me," Blaine said as he stooped down in front of her.

She took her hands away from her face and said, "Blaine, I just know they're going to arrest me for Sandy's death."

"That's crazy talk. What makes you say something like that? We don't even know for sure how she died."

"After my lunch with Mitzi yesterday, as I told you, I got to thinking that her life would make a great subject for a book. You know, fat girl loses weight, has a whole new successful career, finds love in mid-life with a handsome doctor, that type of thing. Sort of like the ugly duckling turns into a beautiful swan theme. What I thought the story needed was some meat."

"You're going to have to spell it out for me, Kat. I'm not connecting the dots here," Blaine said.

"I thought a story like that was kind of dull. It needed some intrigue, what I call meat, if you will. I created a file on my computer about the book and entered all of my thoughts in that file."

"Kat, that doesn't seem like the least bit unusual or anything the police would really be interested in unless they're fans of your books."

She took a deep breath and said, "There's more. After I came back from lunch with Mitzi I not only came up with some ideas for the book, I did some research. That's what has me worried."

"I still don't understand why that's a concern."

"You will when I tell you this. Since Mitzi's an acupuncturist I thought a murder that took place in an acupuncture clinic would provide the intrigue or meat I thought the book needed."

"That's a concern."

"Blaine, it gets worse. I spent a couple of hours looking up ways to kill people as well as all about acupuncture clinics and how acupuncture works."

"You looked up ways to murder someone, Kat?" he asked incredulously.

"Yes, I decided if I was going to write about a murder the book had to have a ring of truth to it."

"Knowing you, I can understand why you did everything you say you did, but I have to agree with you. The police may find all of this quite interesting."

"You're the one who knows about law. Do you think I could be considered a suspect?" she asked as her lower lip began to quiver.

"Unfortunately, yes. That's the bad news. The good news is they can't put the smoking gun in your hand."

"Blaine, now it's my turn, because I have no idea what you're talking about. What do you mean?"

"It means, that yes, they will probably copy all of the sites you visited and the notes you made about your book. They may look at you as a possible suspect, but in order to charge you or anyone else with murder there has to be a nexus. In other words, they have to prove you did something which resulted in Sandy's death. I don't see how they could possibly charge you with murder, other than if you admitted to it, which we both know you won't do, since you weren't responsible for her death."

"Blaine, I'm so sorry for involving you in all of this. How could I possibly know someone would die at Mitzi's clinic?"

"There's a word for people who can tell what's going to happen in the future before it actually does. It's called being 'prescient.' Has this ever happened to you before?"

"No, I know that people who work in law don't believe in coincidences, but honestly, Blaine, that's all this was. Simply a coincidence."

"I'm sure it was, but you have to admit the timing is lousy. I imagine they're taking a long look at you right now."

She twisted the ring Blaine had put on her finger only hours before and said, "Maybe it would be better for you if we put this engagement on hold. I think I'm more of a liability than I am an asset to you at this point."

"Absolutely not. We're getting married, and that's final. What I need to do is get home, call Nick, and tell him what's happened. I want him to help solve this crime and put it at the top of his priority list, but there's something else that concerns me."

"What's that?" Kat asked as she walked him to the door.

"We both know you didn't kill Sandy, but it looks like someone did. That person may know you were present when Sandy died and might think you know something that would help identify the killer. Until the murder is solved, I'd like Rudy to be with you all the time. He may be a gentle giant, but I know you well remember how invaluable he was in saving your life when you became involved in your editor's murder. Can you promise me that?"

"Yes, quite frankly the whole thing creeps me out. I do feel better knowing Rudy is here. Thanks again for getting him for me."

"You're welcome. Now that we've gotten all that out of the way, I think it's only fair that I get a proper kiss from my bride-to-be."

Several minutes later she closed the door behind him and locked it. "Okay, Jazz, Rudy, time to go outside one last time and then off to bed, but first I really need to call Lacie. She needs to hear about this from me before it's on the news. That could really play havoc with her final exams."

CHAPTER FOURTEEN

"Hi, sweetheart," Kat said, "burning the midnight oil getting ready for tomorrow's exam?"

"Yeah, Mom, you know me too well," Lacie said. "It's kind of late for you to be calling. What's up?"

"A lot. First I'll give you the good news. I said yes when Blaine asked me to marry him. What do you think about having a stepfather?"

"I can't think of anyone I'd rather have. Remember when I said when you first met him you'd be crazy not to be interested in him since he's good-looking, rich, nice, and has a prestigious job. Seriously, what's not to like about that? When's the wedding? Am I going to be your maid of honor? Are you going to have a double wedding with Mitzi?"

"Whoa," Kat said laughing, "one thing at a time. First of all, there's nothing not to like about him. I'm thrilled he wants me to be his wife. You know he's never been married, and I consider it a pretty big compliment that I'll be his first wife."

"Think you should add and only wife. Mom, I think you're missing something. My guess is he considers it a pretty big compliment that you'd say yes when he asked."

"I hope so. Let me answer your other questions. The wedding is going to be this fall. We haven't set a date yet. It will probably be at the country club, so no, we won't be part of a double wedding. Lastly, yes, I would like you to be my maid of honor. Oh, I almost forgot to tell you about my engagement ring."

"Is it a diamond? A big one? How did he get one so fast? He must have been pretty sure you'd say yes."

"Slow down, Lacie. I feel like I've stepped back to the time when you were a little girl. You always were curious and asked a million questions. Think that part has stayed with you as you've matured. I can't wait for you to see the diamond he gave me and yes, it's two-carat big. It's just gorgeous. It's a purplish pink heart-shaped diamond. From what he was told the cut, the color, and the fact that it's two carats makes it pretty rare. It's a family heirloom. It was his grandmother's, and she willed it to him. He told me if I didn't like it, he'd get another one. He was very concerned I wouldn't like the setting, because it's not modern, but I think it's gorgeous."

"That is so romantic. I'm envious. Even though I don't have anyone in the wings waiting to give me a diamond, I don't think I'll ever merit a two carat diamond. Does it feel heavy on your finger?"

"Yes, it's taking a little getting used to, but I'm sure I can make the sacrifice," Kat said laughing.

"Mom, all kidding aside, I'm really, really happy for you. I've got the exam tomorrow afternoon and then there are a couple of things I need to do at the Pi Phi house. Okay with you if I stop by tomorrow night?"

"Sweetheart, that's something you never need to ask. You're always welcome, and let me assure you, just because I'm getting married it doesn't mean you're not welcome in your own home. Come to think of it, we've barely discussed whether or not Blaine will move in here or if we'll buy a new house. He has an apartment, and I really can't see moving all my stuff and the dogs into it."

"Mom, if you're going to get new appliances and do some of the other things I've been thinking about, you probably better have him move in. You've got four bedrooms. You can make one of them into an office for him. That would still leave the master bedroom, my bedroom, and your office. Seems like the most sensible thing to do."

"It would probably also be the most sensible thing to do financially."

"Since he's very wealthy, and your books do so well, don't think that's a real big consideration for either one of you. Right?"

"Yes, that's probably true. I just hadn't even considered the future, because I have a little problem I need to talk to you about."

Kat told her what had happened at the acupuncture clinic, her computer research, and the notes she'd made about her next book. She went on to tell her about Nick's visit, the coroner's preliminary report, and concluded by telling Lacie the police had taken her computer, and she was afraid she was being considered as a suspect, although they hadn't exactly said that.

"Mom, that's the craziest thing I've ever heard. Why in the world would you want to kill someone you've never met? I've heard of grabbing at straws, but to think you'd have anything to do with it is just ridiculous."

"Thanks, Lacie, I appreciate your support, but I am concerned. What also worries me is Blaine asked me to marry him today, before he found out I might be considered a suspect in a murder case. It doesn't look too good for the district attorney to have his future wife charged with murder, if the police determine that's what happened. I haven't told him, but I've decided not to marry him until this is solved."

"Mom, you're really overreacting. I've heard about police procedures, and my understanding is they have to go by the book, so I'm not surprised they're questioning you. Since you were there when the woman died, it would make perfect sense to investigate you and everyone else that was there. Then, by the process of elimination, you'll be free and clear. I'll bet this will all be over in a couple of days."

"Lacie, believe me, I wish I shared your optimism. I have to admit I'm pretty shaken, and I feel so sorry for Mitzi. This should be the best time in her life, and instead of planning a wedding, she's trying to clear her name. Doesn't seem fair."

"Have you thought about who could have done it?"

"Nick, Blaine's brother, actually your step-uncle-to-be is doing some investigative work. You remember how much he helped me when Nancy was murdered. Anyway, Mitzi talked to him for quite awhile tonight and yes, between all of us we've identified some suspects. Two in particular stand out. One is the ex-fiancée of Mitzi's husband-to-be. I guess she was furious when he broke off their engagement. The other one is the acupuncture doctor who's also being considered for the same position as Mitzi, that of Assistant Dean of the Acupuncture Department at the university."

"I'm glad you told me, Mom. I sure wouldn't have wanted to hear about this on television, although my time watching it has been severely curtailed for the last week or so. Anyway, try not to worry, and Mom, I'm really glad you're going to write something other than the Sexy Cissy books. Are you going to use your own name or get another pen name?"

"I haven't gotten that far in my thinking. I'll probably use my own name. Actually, given the circumstances surrounding what happened today and the plot I envisioned in the book, it might be better if I used the name Kat Denham rather than my married name-to-be, Kat Evans. That way I could separate Blaine from all of this."

"I think that's an excellent idea. Again, congratulations, and I'll tell Blaine tomorrow night how happy I am for both of you. Oh, Mom, since I'm twenty-one, you can also tell him he won't have to adopt me. Poor guy's not only getting a first wife, he's getting a stepdaughter."

"Knowing the relationship you and Blaine have, I don't think it would bother him in the least, but I'll tell him. Good luck tomorrow. I'll be thinking about you."

"I'd prefer it if you were thinking about how to clear your name if it's determined she was murdered. One more thing, are you keeping Rudy with you? If it was murder, and since you were there when she died, might be a good thing to take him with you wherever you go until this is over."

"Lacie, Blaine and Nick have already lectured me about that, and I've promised both of them I won't even go out the door without Rudy at my side. Does that help?"

"A lot. See you tomorrow."

CHAPTER FIFTEEN

Considering the events that had taken place during the day, Kat slept surprisingly well. She probably would have slept in longer if Jazz hadn't jumped up on the bed and licked her cheek, waking her. "Jazz, thank you for that doggy kiss. I take it you want to go outside."

At the word "outside" Rudy walked over to the bedroom door and looked over his shoulder as if to say, "Me, too."

An hour later, after the dogs were fed and watered, she'd showered, and her morning coffee had been consumed, she sat down at her desk with her iPad. Although she usually wrote her books on her computer, occasionally when she was out of town or she was away from her computer, she wrote on her iPad and then transferred the chapters she'd written to her computer.

She knew Detective Shafer wouldn't understand, but while she was asleep the plot for the book had come alive for her, and before she lost it, like she often did with dreams, she wanted to take it from her memory and get the ideas down in writing. Lost in the newly about-to-be born book, it took a moment before she realized her phone was ringing. She answered it, not recognizing the number.

"Mrs. Denham, this is Detective Shafer. I'd like to come by and talk to you. Are you available now?"

"Yes, will you be bringing my computer back when you come?"

"I am, and that's why I want to talk to you. I'll be there in about fifteen minutes."

She put the dogs outside, feeling she'd be plenty safe with the detective in the house.

Exactly fifteen minutes later, the doorbell rang. Kat looked through the peephole and saw Detective Shafer standing at her front door holding her computer.

"Come in, Detective. Thanks for returning my computer. Would you mind reconnecting it for me? I always get confused when I try to hook the darn thing up by myself."

"Sure, and after I finish, I want to talk to you about what our computer expert found on it." He followed her down the hall to her office, and when he'd finished with the installation he said, "Where would you like to talk?"

"We can do it here in my office. Why don't you sit on the couch, and I'll take the chair?"

"All right. I want you to know we copied several of your files. I'd like to know about the book thoughts you wrote down that we found in one of your files."

"Detective, as soon as you left last night I realized what you were going to find and what it must look like. Let me explain how I came up with the idea and why I visited various web sites dealing with acupuncture and murder."

She explained everything to him, from lunch with Mitzi to researching the sites. When she was finished she said, "I know how this must look. Blaine said that I must be prescient, or be able to know things before they happen. Detective, I've never had anything like this happen in my life. Honestly, it just seemed like a good idea for a book. That's all I know."

He was quiet for several moments. "Mrs. Denham, I've known your fiancé for a long time, and I have nothing but the highest regard for him. When I learned you'd become engaged to him, believe me, it was a huge plus for you. We did a thorough background check on you and you came out squeaky clean. I don't know how authors come up with the plots and characters for their books, but what you've told me sounds entirely plausible. I can't explain how you happened to come up with the idea for a book and then how the events you envisioned for the book actually happened. Our expert was able to determine that you visited the sites the day before Sandy Hendrick died."

"Honest, Detective Shafer, I had no idea that she'd die while I was there. I have no idea how a person can be poisoned and not show any signs of it and then die from it while they're having an acupuncture treatment."

"We're not yet sure of that either. One thing that's in your favor is you didn't visit any sites on poison or high blood pressure medication. If you had, that would definitely put you very close to the top of the suspect list."

"Detective, admittedly, I don't know much at all about those things, although if I'm going to start writing cozy mysteries I probably better find out. Why did you mention high blood pressure medication?"

"We don't know exactly what the substance is that the coroner suspects is a poison. Tests are being run right now. It's not uncommon for people to forget they've already taken their blood pressure medication and take too much, although to take it in doses large enough to cause death would be rare. Right now we're looking at everything."

"I don't know anything about poisons or even which prescription drugs can be dangerous if they're taken in excess. One thing does occur to me, however. I remember Blaine and his brother, who is a private investigator, talking about motive being the first place to look when trying to solve a crime. What motive could I possibly have had?

I'd never seen Mrs. Hendrick until I walked into her treatment room, and she was dead."

"We looked at that, Mrs. Denham, and we found no relationship between you and the decedent, but you must admit, it's all quite coincidental."

"I couldn't agree more. I think it might make a good book, but I have no idea, if it's murder, who the killer will be."

"Mrs. Denham, although you're not an official suspect, don't leave town. If you find out something you think would be of interest to me, don't hesitate to call." He laughed as he stood up, "And if a name comes to you in a dream, I'd like to know about it. If you can solve the death that way, we could probably use you down at the station."

After he left and the dogs were back on their dog beds in her office, Kat spent the next hour transferring what she'd written on her iPad to her computer. She checked it, and all of her files were just as they had been. She knew that while the detective wasn't charging her with Sandy Hendrick's murder, he'd probably be observing her, maybe even following her or having her followed to see if he could come up with a motive.

She shivered thinking about it. Just then her phone rang, and she saw that Nick was calling her. "Good morning, Nick."

"I wanted to give you an update on a couple of things. My team has been busy this morning. One of my researchers was assigned to Matt Hendrick. He's an engineer, and it's well-known that he's what would be called a 'player.' According to one source at the firm where he works, he's had intimate relationships with a number of women at the engineering company. Evidently he's very attractive, and he's been married several times. My researcher talked to a few of the neighbors, and one of them mentioned his wife often went out of town on weekends and when she was gone, a woman usually arrived shortly after she left and spent several hours there."

"Did you find out who the woman was?"

"No, and that's women not woman, but from the description of the latest one my researcher was given, she appears to be a Latina. He said she had black hair, dark eyes, and a good figure. Although he never was able to get a really good look at her, he judged her age to be about forty-five."

"How are you going to find out who she is?" Kat asked, walking idly over to Rudy's dog bed and petting him while she talked.

"I have someone who will follow him after work and see where he goes. Now that his wife is dead he might be a little more open in his relationships."

"I think it's kind of strange he went to work the day after his wife died."

"Yes, but people react to death quite differently, and if he's a player, he may not be mourning his wife's death very much."

"You've done a good job, Nick. Thanks."

"We also did a check on Mitzi Green, and found nothing. She seems as pure as the driven snow. I'm calling her this afternoon. I need some more information on the woman who died. I'd like to know if she was taking any medication, and if so, what it was."

"You might ask her if Sandy Hendrick was taking any blood pressure medicine, because the detective said it was a good thing I hadn't visited sites dealing with poisons or high blood pressure medications. Makes me think he'd found out she was taking blood pressure medication and maybe got too much of it."

"I'll definitely ask her. Thanks for the heads up. I'm also going to be doing some research on Dr. Nguyen."

"I'll be curious what you find out about him, and it may be very small of me, but I hope you find out something that points the finger of suspicion directly at him."

Nick laughed. "Guess you're not perfect after all. My brother speaks of you in such glowing terms I'm glad to see there's a little ordinary human nature in you after all."

"Trust me, Nick, I'm very human. Oh, by the way, did Blaine mention to you the police took my computer last night?"

"Yes, and he also told me what was on it. I know he was pretty concerned."

"I think it's okay. Detective Shafer returned it this morning and said that although they'd copied the pertinent files, at least I didn't have anything on it about poison. He thought it was a very strange coincidence that I'd research something and then what I had researched happened in real life. Hopefully I was able to assure him that it was simply that, a coincidence."

"Kat, sounds like he was playing good cop. Let's hope he doesn't find a reason to play bad cop. If you've got a minute, I have a couple of other things I'd like to talk to you about."

"Sure, other than having lunch with Blaine's secretary and seeing what I can find out about Rex's ex-fiancée, I'm just planning on staying here at home the rest of the day and doing some writing. Blaine's coming over for dinner after he finishes up in court. What else did you want to talk about?"

"I've done a lot of thinking about Sandy Hendrick's death and who might have done it if she was murdered. Obviously, it must have been someone who wanted her dead. That's the first thing that comes to mind. Given the fact her husband seems to be a player; the murderer may be someone who wanted to get back at him by killing his wife. I know it's a stretch, but that's one scenario."

"Actually, I never went beyond who would want to see her dead, much less someone who would do it to get back at someone other than Sandy Hendrick."

"Stay with me for a minute, Kat. Here's another scenario, and one that I'm sure isn't going to make you very happy considering your friendship with Mitzi."

"I'm lost. What do you mean?"

"Well, if someone wanted to get to Mitzi and thoroughly discredit her, what better way to do it than have a patient die while Mitzi was treating her with acupuncture?"

"Yes, I suppose that's true, but if poison killed her, how could Mitzi poison her?"

"I don't have an answer for that, but what about who would want to harm Mitzi? Any thoughts on that?"

"There may be some professional colleagues that are jealous of her, but she never mentioned any to me. There's Rex's ex-fiancée, Dina. I told you I'm going to find out about her at lunch. Evidently Blaine's secretary knows her well. I'll let you know what she has to say about her. The other person is the one I also mentioned to you, Dr. Nguyen. Those are the only two I ever heard her say anything about. Afraid I've got nothing more to add."

"All right. What about you?"

"What do you mean, what about me?" she asked.

"Do you have any enemies? Is there anyone who would want to see you charged with murder?"

"That doesn't make a lot of sense to me. First of all, who would even know I'd be at the clinic at the same time Sandy Hendrick was there? My daughter and Blaine were the only two people who knew I was going there, and since Blaine gave me an engagement ring yesterday, I don't think he'd want me charged with murder, and I sure don't see my daughter, Lacie, doing anything like that.

"We're very close, plus she's in the middle of final exams. Since

I've already been outed as being Sexy Cissy, the author of steamy romance novels, the only enemies I might have had are out of luck on exposing me, because I've already been exposed. Afraid I'm a dead-end."

"Okay. You may not be the target here, but what's concerning me now is that people will know you were there when the woman died. If she was murdered, and certainly that is a very strong possibility now, there's a good chance someone might not want to see you involved any further in this. I think you need to be very careful until this case is solved."

"Nick, you and Blaine, along with Lacie, have already given me the Rudy lecture, so you don't need to repeat it, if that's where you're going. I promised all of you that Rudy would be with me at all times. Okay?"

"Yes, you did make that promise, but out of an abundance of caution, I just want to make sure you understand the seriousness of the situation. I'll probably call you tonight and update you with what I find out this afternoon. You said Blaine's coming over for dinner, right?"

"That I did. As a matter of fact, I need to bake some trout and chill it. It's warm out, so I thought a nice cold trout and cucumber salad with some rolls and gazpacho would be perfect."

"If that's an invitation, I accept," Nick said laughing.

"Don't think your wife and daughter would be very happy about that, but since we're going to be in-laws, I would like to get to know them better. Once this little issue is solved, I'll make a point of having all of you over for dinner."

"Don't think Sandy Hendrick would refer to her death as this little issue," he said.

"You're absolutely right. Once this horrific possible murder has been solved. Does that sound better?"

"Much, and if Detective Shafer pays you another visit, I think it would be best not to use the little issue words."

"I won't. Promise. Talk to you tonight, and Nick, thanks for doing this."

"What's family for?" he asked as he ended the call.

CHAPTER SIXTEEN

"Good morning. You've reached the acupuncture clinic. How may I direct your call?" the voice asked. Nick assumed he was speaking with Rochelle Salazar.

"I'd like to speak with Dr. Green, if she's available. You can tell her Nick Evans is calling."

"One moment, please."

The telephone line was quiet for a few moments and then a voice said, "This is Dr. Green, and I understand that your brother and Kat Denham are getting married. Congratulations on your new sister-in-law. She's a wonderful woman. I called Kat back late last night to apologize for being so emotional earlier in the evening, and she told me Blaine had proposed, and she'd accepted. I'm really happy for her."

"And I'm just as happy for Blaine. I agree with you. She's a wonderful woman, but I have to clear your name and hers so both of you can get married without any dark clouds hanging over your upcoming weddings. If you have a few minutes, I'd like to talk to you. I'm hoping you can answer some questions for me."

"As a matter of fact, you called at a perfect time. I'm in between patients. What would you like to know?"

"First of all, has Detective Shafer talked to you today?"

"Yes, he called and told me his expert had finished with my computer and wanted to know if he should bring it by the office or take it to my home after I get off work. He said his expert had also finished examining my electrode machine. I told him to bring them both to my office and asked him if he'd put the computer in my car for me. I know how to hook it up, so it seemed easier that way. Rex is coming over tonight after we go out to dinner, and he can carry it in. It's pretty unwieldy for me. The detective asked if I'd carve a little time out for him, since he had some questions for me. I told him to come at ten, which he did."

"What did he say about your computer and the electrode machine?"

"He said they'd dusted them for fingerprints and found some, but they couldn't get a match, and he said they could have been anyone's from the janitor to a patient. I told him I was pretty sure they'd find mine, Rochelle's, and Dr. Nguyen's prints on the electrode machine and the box of sterile needles. Evidently they didn't find anything worrisome on the computer, which I think is good news. He said I'd visited a lot of sites regarding news and updates about acupuncture, but that would be perfectly normal behavior for a person who is an acupuncturist."

"What else did he want to know?"

"He wanted me to tell him as much as I could about Sandy's depression, and he questioned me extensively about the patient's medical history sheet Sandy had filled out when she came to the clinic for her first visit. He read it thoroughly and photocopied it.

"I told him everything I knew about her depression. I said that from the way she'd acted recently I thought there was a good chance she was extremely depressed, and although she had some back issues and other miscellaneous aches and pains, the main thing I'd been concentrating on for the last few weeks was her depression."

"Did you feel you were making progress?" Nick asked.

"When someone has had a number of bouts with depression, they usually don't snap out of it immediately. It can take a long time, and the progress can be measured more in inches than feet, if you know what I mean."

"I understand. Did he ask you anything else?"

"Yes. He was very interested in the medications she was taking. She'd listed two when she'd filled out the information sheet. One was a hormone replacement drug she'd been taking for years, and the other one was for high blood pressure. I guess it ran in her family, and she'd had it all her life. She mentioned she'd taken antidepressants in the past, but didn't like the way they made her feel, and that's why she had come to me. She wanted to try a different type of treatment for her depression. The detective was particularly interested in the high blood pressure medication."

"Do you have any idea why?"

Mitzi was quiet for a few minutes. "You know, something just occurred to me from several years ago when I was in school. I remember reading that an overdose of high blood pressure medication can result in death. Do you think that could be why he was so interested in it?"

"I have no idea, but let's go a step further with this, and I'm sure it's probably occurred to the detective. If she was severely depressed and suspected her husband was having an affair, could she have deliberately overdosed on the medicine and committed suicide? Do you think she was suicidal?"

"That thought never occurred to me. I suppose it's possible, but surely the toxicology report would show that, wouldn't it?" Mitzi asked.

"The only thing the toxicology report will show is what she had in her system, not who put it there."

"So what you're saying is she could have committed suicide by deliberately taking an overdose, or she could have died from accidentally taking too much of the medication."

"Yes, but Dr. Green, you're leaving one thing out."

"What's that?"

"Someone could have mashed those pills and put them into her food or drink, and she could have died from ingesting them. In other words, under that scenario, someone murdered her."

"How can it be determined whether she committed suicide or was murdered?" Mitzi asked.

"That's why police departments have detectives. Their job is to figure it all out. I got a call from one of my people who's gathering information on Matt Hendrick. He told me a woman parked in the driveway of the Hendrick's house and took a pail of cleaning supplies into the house about an hour ago. Looks like she's the cleaning lady. I'm hoping he can talk to her, and maybe we can find something out. The one advantage I have over the police and the detectives is I can devote all my manpower to one case. The police don't have that luxury."

"Well, I sure hope you and your people find out enough to clear me."

"Dr. Green, you aren't the only one who wants to see this solved immediately. My future sister-in-law is just as concerned as you are and with some reason."

"Kat? Why would she be concerned, other than for me? The only thing she did was be in the wrong place at the wrong time."

"I take it she didn't tell you about her computer and the book she was getting ready to write."

"No, not a thing. Maybe she didn't want me to worry any more than I am."

He spent the next few minutes filling Mitzi in on why Kat had been looking at certain web sites on her computer dealing with murder and acupuncture and what she planned to write.

"She never told me anything about that."

"I'm not surprised," Nick said. "I imagine she didn't want you to worry any more than you already were. That's why I put an urgent call out to my staff late last night. This case takes precedence over the others we have in the office."

"Thanks, Nick. I'm glad you did. What will you do now?"

"I want to do some research on Dr. Nguyen. My people are watching Matt Hedrick and his house. I just talked to Kat, and she's having lunch with Blaine's secretary who knows Rex's ex-fiancée. I'm hoping she can find something out about her. I think that's pretty much it for now. Kat or I will let you know what we find out. If something occurs to you or you find out anything new, I'd appreciate if you'd do the same for me."

"Absolutely, consider it done, and thanks for the call. I feel better knowing you're helping."

CHAPTER SEVENTEEN

"Matt, it's me."

"I told you never to call me here. What's wrong with you?" he asked in a hushed voice, hoping the engineer in the cubicle next to his wasn't listening. Matt had suspected for a long time that Ronny Jones was living vicariously through Matt's conversations with his lady friends.

Given the fact that his wife died yesterday, he didn't think it would be a good idea to sound like he was being amorous on the telephone. After all, the funeral arrangements for Sandy hadn't even been finalized. He knew people expected him to act like he was trying to shoulder his way through his grief. What they didn't know was he felt like the weight of the world had been lifted from his shoulders.

"Look, I can't talk now. Whatever it is it will have to wait until tonight. I'll come by your house after work." He lowered his voice even further. "Remember, I'm a sucker for pink satin." He ended the call and stood up. Just as he'd suspected, Ronny was sitting as close as he could get to the partition that separated their cubicles. Matt sat down as quietly as he could, smiling at the thought of the upcoming after work liaison and pink satin.

*****

"Excuse me, you speak English?" the paunchy man with the thinning comb over hair asked the young dark-haired Latina woman who was locking the front door to Matt Hendrick's house.

"Un poquito," the short woman with the thick torso answered.

"Well, a little bit's good enough for me," Sol Alpert said. "Un poquito, a little bit, jes' might be enough for me to give ya' this." He pulled a twenty-dollar bill from his pocket. "Lady, all ya' need to do to make this yours is answer a few questions fer me. Think ya' can do that?"

"Si, senor, I think so," she said in a heavy Spanish accent.

"Do ya' mind if we get in yer' car and talk? It's mighty hot standin' out here in the sun."

"Si," she said as she walked to her car and opened the trunk, putting a pail with the cleaning supplies in it. She walked around to the driver's side and opened the door, motioning for him to get in on the passenger side.

"Promise ya' this'll only take a minute. Ya' understann my English?" he asked.

"Si."

"All right. Got a few questions I wanna ask ya'. Take yer' time. First, did Senora Hendrick take any medicine?"

The woman nodded.

"How many medicines?" Sol asked.

She held up two fingers.

"Ya' know why she was takin' 'em?"

"Si. She had the how you say it? High blood pressure. The other was for the woman thing."

"All right. Where'd she keep the pills? They in medicine bottles?"

A car drove past the driveway, and a look of fear crossed the woman's face. "Senor, I no think I should be talking to you. Por favor, leave the car."

"Jes' a couple more questions, and then I will. Were the pills in bottles?"

"No, she put them in her own pretty bottles."

Sol made a mental note that there was no way to know where the decedent had been in her pill cycles, since there was no pill bottle date to show when she'd last renewed her prescriptions. He knew Nick had amazing resources for finding out that kind of information, but Sol was a little skeptical as to whether or not even Nick could get that kind of refill information.

"Ya' like Senor Hendrick?"

A broad smile lit up her dark brown face. "Si. So nice. Sometimes he give me extra money. He says I'm good, and he wished I could live in the house and clean for him every day, but I no think Mrs. Hendrick would like that."

"Why is that?"

She giggled. "One day he tell me how pretty I am and give me a kiss. She walk in. She no like it and told me to finish cleaning and leave. She yell at him. Senor Hendrick, he wonderful man."

Sol handed her the twenty-dollar bill and opened the door of the car. He turned to her and said, "Gracias, Senorita. Appreciate yer' time."

So he gave her extra money for cleanin' the house. Right. My guess is the extra money he gave her was for more than just cleanin' the house, Sol thought as he walked down a block to where his car was parked. *Nick's gonna have a field day with this info. Better call him right away.*

CHAPTER EIGHTEEN

"Nick, it's Sol. Jes' had me a little a talk with the Hendrick's cleanin' lady. Here's what she tol' me." He recounted his conversation with her. "Got anything else fer me today?"

"You did well, Sol. Put the twenty on your expense account. I'll reimburse you. That was good thinking. Any thoughts about Matt Hendrick giving her money?"

"Yeah, but they ain't the kind that are very purty. I'd say he was payin' her for more than cleanin', if you get my drift," he said, snickering into the phone.

"Okay, Sol, I get the picture. I've been playing around with my computer, and I was able to hack into the Swarthout Engineering firm's main frame computer. The engineers' offices are like cubicles. Think it might be worthwhile for you to talk to the man whose cubicle is right next to Matt Hendrick's. His name is Ronny Jones. Did a little research on him, and he seems to have a fondness for the bar across the street from Swarthout Engineering, a joint called Cheers Bar & Saloon."

"That ain't too original, boss. Seems like there's one of 'em in every town."

"Yeah, I know. I was thinking you could meet him when he walks out the door after work today and tell him you're a private investigator and would like to talk to him. Offer to buy him a beer at Cheers. From the information I got, he goes there most nights after work. As a matter of fact, if he's headed that way, you could just wait until he's in there and then buy him a beer and introduce yourself. You decide what's best. I trust your judgment."

"Thanks, that's all well and good, boss, but don't have a clue what this Ronny dude looks like."

"I'm sending a photo of him to your cell phone right now. Got it?"

"Yeah. With that ponytail the dude kinda looks like some hippy dippy guy."

"Could be, but that's not what's important, Sol. What's important is what you can get him to tell you about Matt Hendrick."

"I'm all over it, boss. Thinkin' might be a purty large expense account this month if he's at the bar every night."

"Let him drink all he wants, but I sure don't want you to get pulled over by the police for a DUI and have a drunk driving arrest tied to me. Got it?"

"Boss, yer' hurtin' my feelings. Course I'd never do nothin' like that. Ya' know me."

"Exactly," Nick said drily. "Call me after you talk to him."

*****

Sol watched the entrance of Swarthout Engineering as the workers left the building for the parking lot, finished with another day of work. He'd decided earlier it must be a fairly small firm, since the parking lot was only large enough for about a hundred cars. He spotted the man Nick had sent him a picture of and waited for a moment to see if he was headed towards the parking lot or Cheers.

Evidently Ronny Jones was thirsty, because the bar across the street won.

Five minutes later Sol opened the door to Cheers Bar & Saloon and walked into the dark and smoky establishment. Although there was a county no smoking ordinance for places where food and beverages were served, it was obvious no one paid any attention to it at Cheers. He stood just inside the door for a moment while his eyes adjusted to the dim lighting, and his nose adjusted to the smell of smoke. He saw Ronny Jones seated on a barstool at the far side of the horseshoe shaped bar. By a lucky stroke of fate, the barstool next to him was empty. Sol hurried over to it and sat down, nodding to Ronny as he did so.

"What can I get for you, handsome?" the well-endowed bottle-blond barmaid with the low cut white T-shirt asked as she bent forward and wiped down the area in front of him, leaving very little to the imagination.

"I'll take whatever the favorite is on tap," Sol said.

A moment later she placed a frosted mug filled with beer in front of him. He reached out to get it and deliberately spilled a little on the counter in front of Ronny. "Sorry, man. Durned thing jes' kinda slipped outta my hand fer a moment like it had a mind of its own. Lemme buy ya' one as an apology." He took a couple of cocktail napkins from the stack next to the tip jar and blotted the beer up.

"No, that's not necessary," Ronny Jones said. "I'm fine."

"Nothin' doin'. I insist. My bad. Miss, could you bring my friend here a beer? I kinda made a mess."

A moment later she placed a beer in front of Ronny. He turned to Sol and said, "Thanks, but you didn't have to do that."

"Yeah, well at the end of the day ya' don't need things like that happenin' to ya'. Most days at work are bad enough on their own."

"You can say that again. I work across the street, and it seems they just give me more and more to do."

"Yeah, that's gotta be tough. Seems like the guys who do it right get twice as much work, and the slackers jes' keep on slackin'. That the way it is fer you?" Sol asked in a solicitous manner.

"Yeah, there's a guy in the cubicle next to mine that's always so busy hitting on the ladies he can't seem to make time for work, so I end up doing his job and mine."

"Man, that's rough. Is the guy married?"

"He was until yesterday. Word on the street is that his wife got fed up with all his affairs and decided to end her life. Can't blame her. I'm sure living with someone who never met a temptation he could resist wasn't easy for her. I met her once, and she seemed very nice. Always wondered why he even bothered to get married. After all he'd tried it a couple of times before and wasn't able to make the marriages work. Think he would have learned his lesson. Told me the other day he was having a torrid affair with a woman who had been president of the Paralegal Association. Guess he thought that would impress me."

"I feel for you, man. Has the guy got any kids?"

"Not that I know of, and I suppose that's a blessing. Having a horndog for a dad wouldn't be easy."

"Man, I haven't heard that term for a long time. Kinda remember that means all the guy thinks about is sex."

"That's a perfect description for Matt Hendrick. I can't tell you how many times when I've been trying to complete a project Romeo is having phone sex with some woman. Believe me, makes it pretty hard to concentrate."

"Does his boss know about it?"

"His boss is a woman. Need I say more?"

"Okay, I got the picture." He looked at his watch. "Enjoyed the jaw time. Good luck to ya'. Gotta get home, or I might have some female problems of my own. See ya' around." He took a twenty out of his pocket and said to the barmaid, "Keep the change."

CHAPTER NINETEEN

When Kat spoke with Blaine's secretary, Carly Mason, earlier in the day, they agreed to meet at noon at a restaurant called Olives and Herbs which was only a block from the civic center complex where Blaine's office was located.

The trendy restaurant specialized in Mediterranean food, and from the number of people who patronized it, ethnic food was alive and well in the small university town. As Kat walked along the sidewalk on her way to the door of the restaurant, she saw Carly already seated at a window table and waved to her. A few minutes later Kat hugged her and sat down across from her.

Blaine had often told her that even though Carly was a red-haired beauty that turned heads wherever she went, she was the best administrative assistant he'd ever had. She oversaw his department and made sure it ran smoothly so he could give his full attention to representing the state in prosecuting criminal offenses. It was a win-win situation for both of them. She loved her job, and in a very short time he'd gained a reputation as one of the best district attorneys in the state.

"Kat, before we talk about anything else, I just have to tell you how happy I am for you and Blaine. I swear, that man glows whenever your name is mentioned. When's the wedding? I'm assuming I'll be invited."

"You are definitely on the short list, Carly. Of course you'll be invited. We haven't set a date yet, because I've got a little problem on my hands that I want to take care of first."

"Blaine told me this morning about what happened at the acupuncture clinic while you were there. How bizarre! What a shame you have to even deal with this at a time when all you should be thinking about are your wedding plans."

"Believe me, I wish it hadn't happened, but it did. What I need to do now is clear my name and Dr. Green's. I also intend to find out who killed her, if it turns out she was murdered. Even if our names are cleared, if the murderer isn't found, there will always be a dark cloud hanging over our heads, plus, I don't want Blaine's reputation to be tarnished because of his relationship with me. Fiancée or wife, if there's even a hint of my somehow being involved in Sandy Hendrick's death, it could only hurt him. Do you understand?"

"I do, and I definitely have some thoughts on this, but I think we better order. Even though I'm with the wife-to-be of my boss, if I'm late getting back from lunch, that might not look too good in the eyes of the rest of the department's employees. Let's take a minute to look at the menu and order, although I eat here often enough that I already know what I'm going to have."

"What do you recommend?" Kat asked.

"I love the orange balsamic lamb chops. I think I'll have a salad with a simple olive oil and vinaigrette dressing as well. That will be more than enough for me."

"Sounds wonderful."

"Ladies, are you ready to order?" the handsome dark-haired waiter asked. They gave him their orders. "While you're waiting for your order to come up, please try this toasted pita bread and a little of the lemon garlic olive oil. It's one of our restaurant's specialties. I'll be back in a few minutes with your orders."

Kat broke off a piece of the pita bread and dipped it in the olive oil. "This is fabulous and how very simple. I think I could easily make this at home."

"You're right. You can easily make it at home, but if you eat too much of it I don't advise buying your wedding outfit now, because I can assure you you'll gain a few pounds, and your dress won't fit when it's time for your wedding."

"You're right. I guess I better start thinking in that vein."

"Believe me, I speak from experience. I'm still weaning myself from this stuff," Carly said as she took a piece of the pita bread. "Now let's talk about Dina. What do you want to know about her?"

She was interrupted by the waiter's assistant who served them their salads. "That looks like about the freshest salad I've seen in a long time," Kat said, "and there's nothing I like more."

While Carly and Kat enjoyed their salads, Kat spent the next few minutes telling her about Mitzi's background, how she'd made a mid-life change and how thrilled she was to be marrying Dr. Rex Brown. She also told Carly who she had identified as possible suspects in the death of Sandy Hendrick, if it was determined she'd been murdered.

"So, what I'd like to know from you is whether or not Dina ever said anything about Mitzi, if she ever discussed the fact that Dr. Brown had broken their engagement, and pretty much whatever else you know about her."

"Dina works as the senior paralegal in a very large law firm," Carly said, "and her specialty is medical malpractice. From what I hear, she's very good. I was a paralegal before I became Blaine's administrative assistant, and that's how I met her," Carly said.

"Ladies, enjoy your lunch," the handsome waiter said as he put their lamb chop entrees in front of each of them and drizzled them with a splash of olive oil and balsamic vinegar. They were quiet for a few moments while they ate, and then Carly said, "See why I can't get past the lamb chops?"

"Yes, they're absolutely wonderful, and they don't look that difficult to make. I'll do a search on the Internet and see if I can come up with a recipe that looks like it would work. I bet Blaine would like it."

"I won't take that bet, because I know he does," Carly said. "We've eaten here several times when we needed to get out of the office to discuss certain things. It's one of his favorite dishes.

"Anyway, back to Dina. She was the president of the Paralegal Association. Since a lot of legal work involves doctors, and that's her specialty, she thought it would be a good idea to have a one-day seminar for doctors and paralegals to discuss ways they could help each other. She and Dr. Brown were both speakers at the event, and that's how they met. That was about a year and a half ago.

"I'm not surprised he noticed her, because she's a beautiful woman and very intelligent, but trust me, he's no slouch. Even though he's older, he's not only attractive, but from what I hear he's one of the wealthiest doctors in town, and he's never been married. If you're single that's a huge plus, because it means he won't be bringing any baggage with him, so to speak. At least not any children."

"I don't know if I agree with you about the baggage," Kat said. "Seems to me the older you get the more natural baggage you have. It's just becomes kind of inherent at a certain point."

"Yes, I suppose you're probably right. From what I understand they began seeing each other and became engaged about a year ago. Everything was going well until he fell in love with Dr. Green. I was sitting at Dina's table at our monthly dinner meeting a couple of months ago, and she was furious. She said he'd broken the engagement, but refused to tell her who the woman was he'd fallen in love with. Dina said if she ever found out who it was, she'd do everything she could to make the woman's life as miserable as her life had become."

"Wow! That's pretty strong language."

"Not only that. Dina said she hated her more than she'd hated anyone in her life, and she'd kill her if she knew who it was."

Kat put her fork down and looked at Carly. "Are you sure she said that?"

"Yes. When Blaine told me about the death in Dr. Green's office, my first thought was of Dina. I'm sure she's found out through the grapevine that Dr. Brown and Dr. Green are getting married. Dina's not a warm fuzzy person, and she's made a lot of enemies. Someone who doesn't care for Dina was probably more than happy to tell her who the lucky woman is that's going to marry her ex-fiancé."

Carly continued, "The one thing I can't figure out is how she could possibly murder Mrs. Hendrick. I mean, from what Blaine told me, it looks like the woman died from poison, so how would Dina be able to murder her? She would have had to put the poison in something the dead woman ate or drank before she went to the clinic or did something to her while she was at the clinic, and both of those scenarios seem unlikely."

"I'm as much in the dark as you are, but hate can sure be a powerful motive. Let me mull it over for a while," Kat said as she looked at her watch. "You need to get back to work. Neither one of us wants to get in trouble with Blaine. I was planning on taking care of the check anyway, so why don't you go back to the office? Thanks so much for telling me all of this, and as soon as we set a date for the wedding, I'll make sure Blaine tells you, so you can put it on your calendar."

"I'll not only put it on my calendar, I'll circle it in red with happiness for two of my favorite people."

"Aww, Carly, that's so sweet of you. Go. Talk to you later." She nodded at the waiter to bring the check as Carly walked past the window heading back to work.

CHAPTER TWENTY

Kat had turned her phone off during her lunch with Carly, and when she got in her car she checked her messages. Mitzi had left a message asking her to call as soon as she could.

"This is Kat Denham. May I please speak to Dr. Green?"

"Certainly, just a moment."

"Kat, I'm so glad you called. Where are you?"

"I'm in a parking lot a block from the civic center complex. What's up?"

"Any chance you could come by the clinic? I've got a couple of things I'd like to talk to you about."

"Sure, I'm on my way."

A few minutes later she pulled into the clinic's parking lot and walked towards the clinic's office. "Hi, Rochelle. Dr. Green asked me to stop by. Is she in her office?"

"Yes, this is Dr. Nguyen's day for patients, so she usually does paperwork on the off days. She's expecting you."

Kat walked down the hall to Mitzi's office and knocked on the door.

"Come in," Mitzi said. When Kat opened the door, Mitzi walked over and gave her a hug. "Thank you so much for coming."

"What's wrong?"

"I just had a long conversation with Rex, and he's really concerned for my safety. It seems one of the paralegals who knows Dina called him and told him Dina had told her she'd found out about me. What's worrying him is he wonders if she's behind Sandy Hendrick's death."

"How could she be?"

"The paralegal told Rex that Dina told her she'd found a way to get back at me. She said if she couldn't have Rex, she'd make sure he'd never marry me, because if he did, it would ruin his reputation and his practice. He thought that sounded pretty ominous and wonders if it has something to do with Sandy Hendrick's death, although I don't see how that could be."

"It concerns me, too. I just had lunch with Blaine's administrative assistant, Carly, and she pretty much told me the same thing. We still don't know if Sandy was deliberately poisoned, but if she was, how could Dina have poisoned Sandy and gotten her to die in your office? You're a doctor. Is there some way that could happen?"

"I suppose if she had taken or secretly been given too many high blood pressure pills, it could result in her death. If she voluntarily took too many, that sounds more like suicide, and Dina wouldn't have had anything to do with that, unless she'd given her a reason to commit suicide. Maybe she was having an affair with Sandy's husband and ground up pills and put them in the coffee pot. I don't know. I suppose if she was absolutely intent on poisoning Sandy, there are a number of ways she could have done it. Maybe that's how she was going to get back at me," Mitzi said.

"The two options you just described result in either murder or suicide, but Dina wouldn't be actively doing anything to get back at you if it was suicide. However, if she was having an affair with Sandy's husband, as you suggested, perhaps he told her Sandy was receiving acupuncture treatments from you, and so she decided she could get back at you and ultimately Rex, by casting a cloud of suspicion over you. If that's true, she was probably hoping Rex would call off the wedding. Then again, maybe her affair with him was a coincidence and nothing like that happened."

"That's a little too convenient for me, Kat. Can you think of anything else?"

"Not really, but I do think we need to take a long look at exactly what happens here in the clinic. I know what you do during an acupuncture session, but what about the supplies and the equipment? You said the police took your electrode machine and checked it for fingerprints. Did they check it to see if the calibrations were properly set? If they were too high, could that result in death by electrical shock?"

"In answer to your question, I don't know of a case where it has resulted in death, but I suppose it would be possible, although I think I would have noticed it when I turned it on, and I also think the patient would be very uncomfortable. The thing is, Dina would have had to get into the treatment room where Sandy was going to receive her treatment and reset the calibrations. The only people who have keys to the clinic are me, Dr. Nguyen, and Rochelle. And anyway, I don't see what that has to do with poison."

"I don't either," Kat said. "What about your needles? And don't you swab the part of the patient's body that's going to be treated with an antibacterial solution? Could someone have poisoned your needles or the antibacterial solution?"

"The needles come in sealed packages. No one could tamper with them, and I've been using the same supplier ever since I became a doctor. As far as the antibacterial solution, yes, I suppose a poison could have been introduced into it, but think about this. The antibacterial solution is topical. In other words, it's applied on the exterior of the body, not inside the patient's body. What leads me to believe it was something she ingested is that the detective was extremely interested in Sandy's medications, which tells me the coroner found something in her body, probably in her blood, and not on her exterior body parts. Does that make sense?"

"Yes, and I agree with everything you've said, which takes us back to Sandy having ingested the poison prior to coming here, but was it secretly given to her, or did she deliberately take it? I have no idea how we'd ever find the answer to something like that."

"I agree," Mitzi said. "Kat, I know I may be getting too emotional over this whole thing, but I'm going to be honest with you. You know how drab my past life was. I mean the biggest thing in it was going to the country club for lunch or dinner a couple of times a month. For the first time in my life, I'm really happy, and I'm so afraid if the cause of her death isn't solved soon, Rex will decide there's too much of a scandal surrounding me, and break off our engagement. I know he's done it once before, and I'm worried he could do it again."

"Mitzi, from everything I've heard about the man he's as honorable as they come. I don't know what kind of a relationship you have with him, but I really find it hard to believe he might do something like that. I remember when I told Blaine about hosting your wedding he said he was so glad because Rex talked about you in glowing terms all the time when they played golf. He said Rex was like a different man since you came into his life. He even told Blaine that for the first time in his life he knew what real happiness was. Mitzi, that does not sound like a man who's going to break off an engagement."

"No, I suppose you're right. I'm probably just being overly dramatic. Between you, Detective Shafer, Blaine, and Nick, I'm sure the murderer, if there is a murderer, will be caught. I just wish it was sooner rather than later. I'd prefer to have thoughts of a white wedding dress rather than an orange prison suit. Thanks for coming here and listening to me. I'm sure there are a lot of other things you could be doing, such as writing that book about me," she said pointedly and then grinned.

"Mitzi, how did you hear about that? I was going to surprise you. It just kind of got out of hand before I could tell you about it."

"I found out from Nick. I'm flattered you think my life is interesting enough to become the basis of a novel, but if you're going to be able to predict the future, I'd prefer you made it one of happy things rather than murder."

"Mitzi, I can't predict things. I have no idea how that happened. I've never predicted anything in my life. I was simply looking for some meat, as I call it, something to get people's attention and make them want to continue reading the book, and that's what my fingers wrote. I honestly don't think my brain was engaged while I did it."

"Okay," Mitzi said, "Get out of here and go write a book about me. I want it to be a best seller, but I don't want any of your sexy steamy love scenes in it, although at this point I could probably use the diversion. Can you promise me that?"

"Yes, that I can promise you. Talk to you later."

CHAPTER TWENTY-ONE

Dr. Nguyen remembered the email he'd received from his friend, Duc Trung, urging him to join him in Duc's acupuncture practice in Hong Kong. He'd said how there had been a huge upsurge in traditional Chinese medicine and the fact that acupuncture had been practiced in China for 2,500 years gave it a great deal of credibility in Hong Kong.

Duc had written that even though he, like Dr. Nguyen, had practiced acupuncture in Vietnam, he'd made more money in the first few months he'd been in Hong Kong than he'd made the whole time he'd practiced in Vietnam. He also said how much his family liked the cosmopolitan feel of Hong Kong as well as feeling safe rather than always worried that something might happen in a politicized Vietnam.

Dr. Nguyen had written him back and explained he'd developed a good practice in the United States and was teaching acupuncture at a well-known university. He even mentioned he was being considered for a promotion to the position of Assistant Dean of the Department of Acupuncture and his only competition was a woman who had become an acupuncturist a few years ago.

He'd received a scathing return email from Duc wondering how Binh could even consider taking a position where his competition was a female. He said he'd heard that over sixty percent of the students in acupuncture schools in the United States were women. He went on to say that although more women were now in the workforce in both Vietnam and Hong Kong, still a man with Dr. Nguyen's experience would always be promoted over a woman and should be. He wondered why Dr. Nguyen would work for someone who would even consider promoting a woman over a man.

Dr. Nguyen had written him back, explaining that even though he agreed with Duc, there were cultural differences involved. He told Duc he would think about his offer and asked him when he needed an answer.

Dr. Trung had responded that he was getting Dr. Nguyen's office ready, but there was no absolute deadline, because he knew eventually Binh would want to come to Hong Kong. Duc had also written that if it was him, and if Binh chose to stay in the United States, and he really wanted the job of assistant dean, he'd find a way to get rid of his female competition.

Dr. Nguyen had sat at his desk in the clinic for a long time thinking about what Duc had written. If he were to discredit Dr. Green, what would be the best way to do it, without causing problems for him? He really did like living in the United States. His parents were elderly, and his father was in ill health in Vietnam, but Binh had no desire to go back there to live. He was glad to have escaped from under the heavy thumb of the Communists. The friends he corresponded with said they never knew from day to day whether they would be taken away by the government authorities on some trumped-up charge.

If he did something to discredit Dr. Green, it would have to be done in such a way that he could never be suspected of doing it, and it would have to be something major in order to make Dr. Warren remove Dr. Green's name from consideration.

Binh began to pull up sites on the Internet dealing with acupuncture and toxicology until he found what he was looking for. He read it several times, knowing there was information in it that could discredit Dr. Green, but what was the best way to do it?

He was deep in thought when his cell phone rang. It was his wife reminding him they were expected at his nephew's birthday party in thirty minutes. She told him whatever he was doing it could wait, because he'd promised his nephew he would be there for his twenty-first birthday celebration. Binh had completely forgotten about it. He jumped up, grabbed his coat, locked the door, and hurried to his car.

*****

She noticed that the light was on in the doctors' office at the clinic and used her key to get in. She walked into his office and saw he'd forgotten to turn off his computer. She sat down and read what was on the page he'd been reading, and then saw he'd also pulled up information on the acupuncture points that were most susceptible to poison. She took a flash drive out of her purse and downloaded the displayed information onto it. She turned off his computer, locked the door, and said a silent prayer of thanks that she'd driven by the clinic on her way home from the gym. This could very well solve the problem. Sometimes it seems things just fall into your hands for no reason at all and when they do, you have to be ready to take advantage of them.

CHAPTER TWENTY-TWO

Kat looked at the monitor on her phone and saw that the call was from Mitzi.

"Must be my lucky day, Mitzi. I'm hoping you have some thoughts on the book, and by the way, I really think there should be at least one steamy scene in the book that involves you. Who would ever know the main character in the book is you? I've given you a new name."

"Sorry, but I've been a little too busy talking to Detective Shafer to have any thoughts about the book. Let's put that on hold for the time being."

"Did he stop by or call or what?" Kat asked. "Does he have any news about Sandy?"

"He called. Yes, he did have news about Sandy, and I really don't know where to go with it. He said that the coroner found a large concentration of Digoxin in Sandy's body, and her case is definitely being treated as a murder. Are you familiar with that drug?"

"No, I've never heard of it, but you're the doctor, not me. Tell me about it."

"I vaguely remember studying about it in one of my courses when

I was in acupuncture school," Mitzi said. "I couldn't remember exactly what it was, so I looked it up on Wikipedia. Here's what they had to say about it, and I quote: 'Digoxin toxicity may occur in individuals who take excessive amounts of the drug Digoxin in a short period of time or in individuals who accumulate high levels of digoxin during an ongoing chronic treatment. Digoxin (derived from foxglove plants of the genus Digitalis) is a medication prescribed for individuals with heart failure and/or atrial fibrillation." She continued, "I also remember that it's so potent it's only used in emergency rooms in hospitals. Doctors don't have it in their offices."

"Okay, but I'm not tracking with you. Help me out. What did Detective Shafer have to say about it?"

"He asked if I was familiar with the drug. I told him I vaguely remembered studying it, but no, I was not familiar with it. He asked if I had the drug here at the clinic, and I told him no."

"Well, if you don't have the drug there, and from what I remember, they did a pretty thorough search of your office, doesn't this mean that you're no longer a suspect."

"Not really. He didn't say it outright, but there was an underlying disbelief in his voice."

"Could Sandy have been taking the drug and accidentally overdosed on it, or do you think she was given an excessive amount by an unknown third party, in other words, murdered?"

"There's no reason for her to be taking it. Number one, no doctor in his right mind would prescribe that along with the blood pressure medication she was taking. That would produce a lethal soup in the body and almost certainly lead to death. Patients who are given Digoxin have heart failure and/or atrial fibrillation, and as far as I know, like I said earlier, it's only used in critical situations like when a person needs it when they're in the emergency room at a hospital. No, there's no way she would have been prescribed the drug."

"Well, if the coroner's findings are correct, someone got it and administered it to her. Is the coroner going to list that as the cause of death?"

"Detective Shafer didn't tell me that outright, but it was kind of implicit. Kat, this makes it ever so much more difficult to solve the mystery of who killed Sandy. I also looked up to see if an individual could purchase Digoxin without first getting a prescription from a doctor, and I found out it's readily available online. I saw a bunch of sites where it's available in Canada. Seems nuts to me because someone would need extensive medical knowledge to use it properly, and it is definitely not a drug that should be administered by a patient acting as an armchair doctor."

"What keeps going through my mind is how it was given to her," Kat said. "If anyone can get it online by simply buying it in Canada, that's one thing, but it's a lot more difficult to figure out how someone gave it to her and why, unless murder was the intent."

"I feel certain she didn't order it. She told me once she hated to take pills. She even said she'd walk around all day with a headache rather than take an aspirin. Sandy was not the type of person to buy and take that type of medication, and why would she? No, the use of Digoxin definitely speaks of murder, not suicide. There was absolutely no reason for her to voluntarily take that particular drug."

"Well, Mitzi, other than knowing that she died from it, we're kind of back to square one. Who gave it to her? Seems like an endless loop."

"I agree. I just wanted to let you know the latest in the case. I've got several more hours of work here, and then I'm meeting Rex for dinner. He's really worried about me and all of this business about Sandy's death. I sure wish we could find the murderer and get this behind us. Anyway, I'll talk to you tomorrow."

CHAPTER TWENTY-THREE

Kat spent the next hour making notes about her new book. She knew it was a dicey thing to do, because readers often wanted an author to continue writing in the same genre, particularly when they felt like they knew the characters that had been developed earlier in a series. To introduce them not only to a set of new characters, but also a completely different type of book, was a definite risk. She knew it could bomb, but she was at a point in her writing career where she was willing to take the risk. She sighed deeply, hoping the risk would be worth it.

Time to fix the cold trout salad. Glad I thought to have it. It's uncommonly warm for a late spring day, so it should be perfect.

"Outside, guys," she said to Jazz and Rudy. "I appreciate your help, but the last time I made it and walked into the kitchen, you, Rudy, had your paws on the counter, and were licking the skin of the trout. Don't want to revisit that scene," she said laughing as she shooed the two dogs out the screen door and told them to stay.

She baked the trout, let it cool, prepared it for the salad, and then refrigerated it. She chopped the vegetables, and as she'd done numerous times before, wished once again she had a sous-chef to do all of her chopping. She assembled the salad and put it in the refrigerator to chill until it was time to serve dinner. She didn't feel like making biscuits from scratch, so she took a tube of readymade biscuits from the refrigerator and placed them on a cookie sheet. Lastly she prepared a cantaloupe, blueberry, and strawberry salad, thinking she'd add a dollop of blueberry yoghurt on top when she served it.

Just as she was finishing up, the doorbell rang. The dogs ran through the makeshift doggie door and waited for her to open the front door for Blaine. When she did, he walked in, kissed her, and petted each of the dogs.

"Blaine, you're the smart one here. Would you tell me how when the dogs are outside in the back yard they know that the ringing doorbell means you're on the other side of the front door?"

"I wouldn't say I'm the smart one, because you can hold your own with anyone, but I will say I have a theory. I've read that dogs have the capacity to hear two or three times better than humans. I think they know the sound of my car, and it registers with them that when that sound is heard, I'll be here, and I'll probably give them a scratch on the head or pet them.

"It's similar to the Pavlov conditioning thing. I'm sure you remember about it from a science class. It finally got to the point when Pavlov entered a room his dogs would start salivating. This isn't all that different, since I've also been known to give Jazz and Rudy treats. I've heard it said that dogs can't remember, and that's why you shouldn't scold a dog when you're trying to housebreak them unless you catch them in the act. I don't buy into that theory. I think they remember just about everything."

"I have to agree, but I think their sense of smell is just as acute. There's no doubt in my mind that when I took some trout out of the refrigerator earlier today, Rudy's memory of licking it the last time I made it kicked in. He and Jazz were outside, and he came running to the door the minute I took it out of the refrigerator. Don't think that was happenstance."

"I agree, now are you going to offer me a glass of wine?"

"I'll do you one better. I've already opened a nice bottle of chardonnay, and it's chilling in the refrigerator. I'll let you pour while I get things ready for dinner. How's that for service?" Kat asked.

"Pretty good. I'm just hoping it doesn't end when we get married."

"Think I can promise that," Kat said grinning as she accepted a glass of wine from him. Just then Kat's cell phone rang and she said, "Darn it, I wish people wouldn't call at the dinner hour. Oh well, it's your brother. I better take this call."

"Hi, Nick. Did you have a productive day? Find out anything that will help Mitzi and me? You did? Blaine's here. I'm going to put you on speakerphone, so I don't have to repeat what you tell me."

Nick proceeded to tell them about Sol and what he'd found out from Ronny and the cleaning lady.

"Wow, so Sandy's husband could possibly be having an affair with Dina, Rex's ex-fiancée? That seems almost too coincidental, don't you think?" Blaine asked.

"Yes, it does, and I'm not sure where you want to go with all of this, Kat. It does seem that Dina might have had the ability to put Sandy's blood pressure medicine in a substance that Sandy could have taken. Of course, if she did it with Matt's help, that makes him an accessory to the murder. The problem is proving it."

"Nick, have you talked to Mitzi or the coroner this afternoon?" Kat asked.

"No, why?"

"Detective Shafer called her and told her that the coroner found large amounts of Digoxin in Sandy's body, and that's what killed her."

Blaine looked at Kat with raised eyebrows. After a moment Nick said, "That means she didn't die from an overdose of blood pressure medication, right?"

"That's pretty much what we understand. From the research Mitzi did after he called, the drug is used almost exclusively in emergency room situations in a hospital and wouldn't have been given to Sandy as a prescription, however, it is for sale on the Internet," Kat said.

"Isn't everything?" countered Nick. "Kat, where do you think that leaves us?"

"I don't know. Blaine, please feel free to chime in. Nick, what are your thoughts?"

"I suppose Dina and/or Matt could have done it, but it doesn't seem as likely given that she died from digoxin toxicity. The tablets or what form it was in could have been purchased over the Internet and somehow given to Sandy in a drink or in her food. I find that unlikely. The blood pressure medication seemed far more plausible to me," Blaine said.

"I agree," Nick said, "but here's something else I just received as a text from the man I have watching Matt Hendrick that I find very interesting. Matt left work, pulled into the driveway of a house that isn't his, and then used a garage door opener and drove into the garage of this house. He put the door down as soon as his car was in the garage. The address is 473 East Mesa Drive. Ring a bell, Kat?"

She thought for a moment and then gasped. "Isn't that Rochelle Salazar's address, the receptionist that works at the acupuncture clinic?"

"Bingo, you win. Yes, so what do you make of that?" Nick asked.

"Quite frankly, I have no idea. From what Sol said it sounds like Matt Hendrick is a serial skirt chaser, but with Rochelle? I wonder how they ever met? I need to ask Mitzi if he ever went to the clinic with Sandy. Maybe that's how."

"Put that on your list of things to do, but what interests me more than anything else is that for the first time we have a nexus. Matt is married to Sandy. Sandy goes to the acupuncture clinic to be treated. Matt is presumably either a very good friend or is having an affair with Rochelle, who works at the acupuncture clinic. We can all figure that out, but the problem is how was Sandy poisoned? Even if we can put all of them at the clinic, not one thing, from what I understand from you, Kat, and from Mitzi, leads to the Digoxin trail. Am I right?" Nick asked.

"Yes, if it was either one of them, how did they do it? That's the million-dollar question," Kat said. "I'll call Mitzi after we eat and see if she can think of anything, given this new information. As always, Nick, thanks. Talk to you later."

As she hung up, the doorbell rang. "I'll get it, Kat. Stay where you are." Jazz and Rudy accompanied Blaine to the door wagging their tails.

"From the looks of the dogs' tails, I think it must be Lacie," Kat said. "She wanted to stop by, see my ring, and talk to you."

He opened the door and gave Lacie a big hug. "I seriously thought about calling you and asking for your permission before I proposed to your mother, but I didn't get around to it. Things happened a little faster than I expected. I hope you don't mind."

She pushed Blaine away and looked up at him, "Are you kidding? I couldn't be happier, but there is one problem," she said laughing. "Mom comes with some baggage in the form of me."

He hugged her again and said, "Actually I don't consider you to be baggage, I consider you a plus. Your mom's in the kitchen, but I think you better stop where you are for a minute, because you have two dogs clamoring for special attention from you."

"Hi guys, here's pats for both of you, now I really want to see this ring Mom told me about." She walked toward the kitchen followed by Blaine and the dogs.

When she got to the kitchen she found Kat hamming it up and moving her ring finger back and forth so the rays from the setting sun would catch the ring and send colorful prisms of light throughout the kitchen. She paused, so Lacie could get the full effect and then began moving her finger around again. "Mom, that is a serious knuckle duster!" She turned to Blaine and said, "You done good, Blaine, you done real good!" She walked over and kissed him.

"Seriously, I am so happy for both of you," she said. "I would love to stay, but I'm down to one more exam, and I think there's a good chance I can make the dean's list this semester. Anyway, for that to happen I need to get back to the sorority house and study. I'll call you tomorrow after I finish my test, and we can start planning what you're going to do to the house to get ready to host Mitzi's wedding."

"Kat, it just occurred to me we've never really discussed where we're going to live when we're married. I know I said I would move in with you and help you and Lacie with the things you were going to get to spruce the house up before Mitzi's wedding, but that was before we got engaged. Have you given it any thought?" Blaine asked after he closed the door behind Lacie.

"I haven't, but Lacie has. She thinks we should live here, because she's insisting I get new appliances and some other things for the house. Somehow I have a feeling before this is over a lot of things are going to be redone. She also mentioned that since the house has four bedrooms, we could make one of them into a study for you. How does that sound?"

"Perfect, but as I mentioned before, I do have one request."

"What?"

"Since I'm going to be living here, I really do want to go shopping with the two of you, if you wouldn't mind my input," he said.

"I remember you said you'd like to go with us, and I think that's perfectly reasonable. You definitely should have a say in this."

"Think I also need to bring my checkbook as well. At some point we're going to have to have the financial talk," Blaine said.

"Yes. I know you have a large trust fund. I agree. I have no problem with a prenuptial agreement."

"Kat, I don't recall ever saying anything about a prenuptial agreement. I'm thinking whatever is mine is yours and vice-versa."

"Blaine, that doesn't sound fair to you. You're the one with the money. What if, heaven forbid, something happened to you not long after we were married. I shouldn't get all that money."

"Kat, there are some things I'm kind of old-fashioned about. Not niggling over money is one of them. And if something happens to me, oh well. And if something happens to both of us, then Lacie won't have to worry about her future. Won't be saying this very often, but this is one subject I'd like to consider closed. The only other relative I have is Nick, and he inherited as much as I did. He certainly doesn't need my money. Now, I'm starving, let's eat."

CHAPTER TWENTY-FOUR

"Kat, that was fantastic. I've never had a chilled trout salad before. In fact, the only trout I've had always tasted a whole lot stronger than what was in that salad, plus it had to be super healthy."

"And low calorie. Since everyone I know is watching their calories, me included, I'm always on the lookout for tasty low-calorie meals. I'll definitely make it for you again. If you'll give me a hand with the dishes, we can sit down afterwards and start making some wedding plans. I think I'm brain dead on this whole murder thing."

"Sure," he said pushing his chair back from the table and stacking their plates to take them to the sink. "I've been thinking about the country club and our wedding. You know I'm past president of the Men's Golf group there, and I have a lot of friends in it. I'd like to invite quite a few of them, and if I do that this wedding may be a little larger than we'd originally thought. I'm planning on having Nick as my best man and that's it. Thought we could keep the wedding party somewhat small since other than Lacie and Nick and his family, we really don't have any close relatives."

"Sounds good to me. I think I mentioned Lacie has already asked if she could be my maid-of-honor. Naturally, I said yes. You're much more active in the club than I've been, so I assume you'll have a lot more people at our wedding than I will. Don't forget, now that you're the district attorney, you're probably also going to have to ask some people just for political reasons."

He grimaced and said, "I hadn't thought of that, but you're probably right. Maybe we should just elope to Las Vegas and have Elvis marry us."

"Somehow I don't think either Lacie or Nick would be very happy with that decision. No, we'll do it the old-fashioned way, but even though you've never been married before, I'm not wearing some wedding gown with a trail and a veil that you have to raise to kiss me. We're a little long in the tooth for that."

"Agreed. I think I hear your phone. Can you get it, or do you want me to get it?"

"I've got it," she said wiping her hands on a dish towel. A moment later she said, "Mitzi, I think we've talked more today than we have in months. What's new?" She listened for a moment and said, "Of course. Come on over. Blaine's here, and I'm very curious to look at what it is you want to show me. See you in a few minutes."

*****

"Jazz, Rudy, on your beds," Kat said when the doorbell rang. She opened the door. "Come in, come in. You must be Rex. I'm Kat, and I'm so glad to finally have the opportunity to meet you."

Blaine walked across the room and shook Rex's hand and kissed Mitzi on the cheek. "So what brings you two over here?" Blaine asked.

A grim-faced Mitzi answered, "Kat, can the four of us go to your office? I want to show you something, but first I need to tell you how I came to get it."

"Sure, and I have to say, you've certainly whetted my curiosity," Kat said as she led the way to her office. "Blaine, help me get a couple of chairs from the kitchen, and then we can all have a place to sit down."

When they'd brought in the chairs she said, "Okay, Mitzi, now that we're all here, want to tell Blaine and me what's going on?"

Mitzi took a deep breath and began to speak, "When I talked to you a few hours ago, I mentioned I had a lot of paperwork to catch up on at the clinic. I think I told you I was going to meet Rex for dinner. A half hour before it was time for me to meet him I decided I'd done enough for today and thought I'd get to the restaurant a little early, so I could freshen up. Because I was the last person to leave the clinic, it was my responsibility to lock the front door. I keep the key for the door in a special place in my purse, but I couldn't find it. I turned my purse upside down trying to find the key, but it was nowhere to be found." She turned to Kat and said, "I'm sorry, but is there any chance you could get me a glass of water?"

"Sure, I'll be right back. Hold whatever you were going to say until I return." A few minutes later she returned with the water.

Mitzi took a big swallow from the glass and said, "I knew I couldn't leave the clinic unlocked for the night with things like our computers in there, and I didn't know what to do. I was on the verge of calling Rex and asking him to go to my house and see if he could find the key to the clinic when I remembered we keep a spare key in the reception desk, just for this type of an emergency." Clearly agitated, she took another sip of water from the glass.

"Mitzi, take your time. Whatever it is, I'm sure it's not critical to the case, so you don't need to hurry."

"Hate to say you're wrong, Kat, but in this case you are. What I'm going to tell you is absolutely critical to the case."

Kat, Blaine, and Rex all leaned forward in anticipation of what Mitzi was going to say. "I looked in the bottom drawer at the back where we kept the key under a stack of papers and in what looked like a box of pens. I'd made the decision a long time ago that I didn't want the emergency office key very visible in case someone tried to find it. No one would think to look inside a box of pens. When I reached for the box, I noticed something under it. I pulled the thing out, and it was a flash drive. The last time I'd used the emergency key to the office several months ago the flash drive had not been there. I'm absolutely certain of that. I was curious what was on it and why it was even there."

"Mitzi, who has access to the reception desk?" Blaine asked.

"Dr. Nguyen, Rochelle, and me. Since the desk drawers were never locked, theoretically, anyone could have opened that drawer and put the flash drive in there."

"But from the way you're saying this, it sounds like you think it was put there by one of them, is that right?" Kat asked.

"Yes, and I want you all to see what's on it. Rex hasn't even seen it. I called him at the restaurant and told him to meet me at your house. Here goes," she said inserting the flash drive into the computer.

There was absolute silence in the room as they watched the computer screen for approximately four minutes. When it was over, Mitzi removed the flash drive and said, "Well, what do you think?"

Rex was the first to speak. "Obviously someone was doing research on poisons and with the amount of research done on Digoxin, it seems that's the one they were most interested in. I know a little about the drug, and if it's not administered properly, it can result in death. The other stuff seemed to be about certain acupuncture points, but that's your area, Mitzi."

"Rex, I haven't had a chance to tell you this, because you were in surgery this afternoon, but I had a conversation with Detective Shafer this afternoon..." Mitzi told him about the coroner's finding and how the detective had questioned her regarding the drug known as Digoxin.

"Okay, Mitzi, it definitely seems that someone was researching Digoxin, but what does that have to do with the acupuncture research on the flash drive?"

"Believe me, that's all I've been thinking about since I saw it, and I have a theory. For the first time I think I know how Sandy was murdered."

"Mitzi, before you begin, I think Detective Shafer needs to be informed of this, particularly if you have a theory. Could you hold off telling us until he gets here, assuming I can reach him?" Kat asked.

Blaine spoke up. "I think Kat's right. This is his case, and it seems to be going into some areas that are a far cry from the usual murders that are committed by using a knife or a gun. Kat, I definitely think you should give him a call and see if he can come over here right away."

"I hadn't thought about it, Kat, but yes, please call him," Mitzi said. Kat went down the hall, and they heard her talking on her phone. A few minutes later she walked back into the office and said, "He's on his way. Blaine, would you mind answering the door when he gets here? He respects you more than he does me."

*****

"Dr. Green, Dr. Brown, Mr. Evans, Mrs. Denham, thanks for including me in this meeting, although I don't really know what it's all about," Detective Shafer said after he'd taken a seat in Kat's office.

"Mitzi, why don't you tell him everything you've told us?" Kat said. They listened as Mitzi recounted the events of the evening.

"Before I go any further, Detective, I'd like to show you what was on the flash drive. The others have already seen it, but I'd like you to be on the same page as them."

They were quiet while the detective watched the computer screen as the research sites on Digoxin and acupuncture flashed up. When it was finished, he turned to Mitzi and said, "I know what I just saw, but I don't understand the connection between Digoxin, acupuncture, and the case at hand."

"I have a theory, Detective, and it is strictly that. I haven't figured a lot of it out, but this is what I'm thinking. What if someone put Digoxin on the tips of the needles I used on Sandy Hendrick? If Digoxin was on them, and I used the electrode machine to stimulate the needles, it seems to me the poison would go into the body faster. Secondly, a couple of the charts on the flash drive deal with the acupuncture points that are the most susceptible to immediate entry into the blood stream and the heart.

"Unfortunately, I was treating Sandy, as I've already told you, for depression, and the acupuncture points on the meridians an acupuncturist uses to treat that disorder would be the very ones that would act the fastest and pretty much go directly to the heart. In other words, if someone put Digoxin on the needles I used to treat Sandy and they were stimulated and put into those specific points, it could result in death." She sat back and took a deep breath.

Everyone started to speak at once. Rex held his hand up. "Mitzi is absolutely correct on her assessment of Digoxin. It definitely could be responsible for Sandy's death, but what I don't understand is how it could be put on the needles."

"I think I can answer that question," Kat said. "One time when I was having a treatment I was watching Mitzi open the packets of needles. They come in individual packets which are sealed with something like an adhesive. I noticed that she opened them very easily. I'm sure they're packaged that way in order to make it easy for the acupuncturist to get them out and not waste a lot of time. Since recycling is such a big deal these days I was curious if the packets could be resealed and reused. It seemed kind of like a waste to throw all that paper away. After my treatment I took one out of the waste basket, and I was able to easily reseal it."

"Kat, that doesn't seem very smart, I mean you could have really hurt yourself if you jammed a needle into your finger," Blaine said.

"No, all the used needles go into a special hazardous waste container designed just for them, and I'm assuming they're gotten rid of when the container is full. Would that be right, Mitzi?"

"Absolutely. Each needle is only used once, and then it's safely disposed of."

Detective Shafer took his glasses off, got a handkerchief from his pocket, and cleaned them. "Dr. Green, let me be clear about this. You're saying that digoxin could have been put on the needles you inserted into special points on the decedent, and because of where you inserted the needles with the poison on them, it could have resulted in death. Is that correct?"

"Yes, and based on what Kat just said, with the needles in sealed packets, I would never have suspected they'd been tampered with."

"All right," Detective Shafer said, "Theoretically, that could explain how she died and why there were no signs of foul play. Doctor, correct me if I'm wrong, since I've never had an acupuncture treatment, but I'm assuming the needles are so thin it would be very hard to determine even where they'd been inserted into the body."

"You're absolutely right," Mitzi said. "After an acupuncture treatment there are almost no signs on the body of where the needles have been placed during the treatment. In the past, before the needles became so thin, patients were advised not to shower for two hours after the treatment or until the microscopic holes in the skin closed, but now it's really not an issue."

"Well, if your theory is correct, and I have to say it's very plausible, there are two things to consider. Who put the poison on the needles, and who put the needles in the room where you treated Mrs. Hendrick?"

Kat spoke up. "I think we can use a process of elimination here. I don't think there's any way that Dina or Matt Hendrick could have done it, given the fact they'd have to have been physically present at the clinic, and I'm sure you would have found that strange, Mitzi."

"Definitely," she answered.

"So if we eliminate them, and we have to eliminate me, because I was never in her treatment room, then it leaves two suspects who would have had the knowledge and the ability to get into the treatment room."

"And those are?" Blaine asked.

"Dr. Nguyen and Rochelle, but there's something else that's critical in this scenario. Mitzi, how is it determined which patient goes into which room? Here's why I think it's critical. Someone had to put those needles into the room where Mrs. Hendrick was going to be treated." She turned to Mitzi and said, "Do you schedule, say the night before, who will go in what room or is it just whatever room is available when someone comes into the clinic for their treatment?"

Mitzi was quiet for several minutes realizing that with her answer she was effectively accusing someone of murder. She looked at the others who were waiting expectantly and slowly began to speak. "As much as I'd like to say it was Dr. Nguyen, I don't think it could have been. He would have no way of knowing which room Sandy would be put in. Rochelle is the one who determines which patient goes in which room. As much as I hate to believe it was her, I don't think it could have been anyone else. If she is having an affair with Matt Hendrick, as we've been led to believe by what Nick's employee saw today, that could be the motive."

"Wait a minute," Detective Shafer said. "What's this about an affair between Rochelle and Matt Hendrick? I know nothing about that."

Kat filled him in on what Sol, the investigator who worked for Nick, had found out, as well as his employee who had observed Matt driving into Rochelle's garage.

The burly detective was quiet for a moment as he absorbed the information, then he said, "Let's get back to those needles for a minute, Dr. Green. The needle box was dusted for fingerprints, and we found yours, Dr. Nguyen's, and Rochelle's on them. Is that normal?"

"Yes, Dr. Nguyen and I rotate treatment days and Rochelle restocks the needle boxes for us."

"Dr. Green, do you make notes on the patient's chart as to how many needles you inserted and where?"

"Always. Each condition for which we provide treatment has a prescribed number of needles, kind of like a recipe. We're also required to keep very detailed and accurate records, particularly for patients who are covered by insurance."

The detective leaned forward in his seat. "If it's Rochelle, she could easily find out how many needles you would be using on Mrs. Hendrick and could put just that number of them in a box. Is that correct?"

"Yes, that's correct."

"Dr. Green, do you remember anything special about that particular box of needles?"

"Yes. I remember thinking I needed to tell Rochelle to get a new box, because I used the last of the needles on Sandy." She sat back and said, "Everything fits, now the problem is, how do we get her to admit she was the one who murdered Sandy?"

"I don't think she'll admit it voluntarily, but while you were talking I thought of a way we could catch her," Kat said. She spent the next ten minutes telling them about it.

When she was finished, Blaine stood up and said, "Kat, please don't even consider it. That's way too dangerous for you."

"Actually, Mrs. Denham," Detective Shafer said, "it's an excellent plan. I promise you'll have all the police protection you need."

"I have the distinct feeling that what I think about this hare-brained scheme doesn't matter, so Kat, will you do me one favor?" Blaine asked.

"What's that?"

"I'd like Rudy to be with you."

CHAPTER TWENTY-FIVE

The following morning promptly at 9:00 when the acupuncture clinic opened, Kat called and when the phone was answered, said, "Good morning, Rochelle. It's Kat Denham. I don't know what's wrong with me, but I'm so depressed I could barely get out of bed this morning. I remember Mitzi telling me once she's had good success treating people with depression. Although she's only treated me for my backaches before, I want to see if acupuncture can help with my depression. Could you schedule an appointment for me this afternoon?"

"I'm sure we can fit you in. Let me look at the computer and see what I have open." She was quiet for a few minutes. "Mrs. Denham, she can see you at 4:00 this afternoon. Actually her last appointment for today left a message on our answerphone that he needed to cancel his appointment, so 4:00 is available. Will that work for you?"

"Yes. Oh, by the way, I understand you've been seeing Matt Hendrick. Certainly was convenient that his wife died, wasn't it, but you don't need to worry. Mum's the word as far as I'm concerned. I won't say anything to the detective who's investigating the case. See you this afternoon."

After Kat ended the call, Rochelle sat in stunned silence, simply staring at the phone, not believing what she'd just heard.

How could she possibly know I'm seeing Matt? I wonder what else she knows? What did she mean by saying it was convenient his wife died? I wonder if she knows about the needles? I wonder if she's talked to anyone?

Even though she was churning inside, on the outside Rochelle acted as if nothing had happened. She greeted the patients, took them to their treatment rooms, restocked supplies as necessary and did what she normally did in the acupuncture clinic. She spent the rest of the morning finalizing a plan in her head and at noon, she walked down the hall to Mitzi's office. She said, "I have this sick feeling I left the burner on when I cooked my oatmeal this morning. I'm going home for lunch and double check."

"That's fine. My last patient for this morning just left, and I don't have another one until 2:00 this afternoon. Take your time."

I'll take my time, all right. I'm just glad when I originally treated some of the needles with Digoxin I made extra ones. You never know when some poisonous needles will come in handy. From what I read the Digoxin should still be effective. Glad I thought to put them in the back of my linen closet rather than throw them out. I think I need to call Matt and tell him what I've done. After I take care of Mrs. Denham, I'll pick him up at work, and we can leave town. He always said how much he'd like to live with me. Well, now's his chance.

*****

At 2:00 Kat's phone rang and she saw Detective Shafer's name on her screen. "Good afternoon, Detective. Are you calling to wish me good luck?"

"No, but I think you may need it. I believe your proposed sting operation is going to work. I just had a call from Matt Hendrick. When I spoke with him the day of the murder, I questioned him extensively about his wife's prescriptions and everything else. I told him that although I didn't consider him a suspect, I didn't want him to leave town until the case was solved."

"That's pretty much what you told me, too," Kat said.

"That's true, but when he called he told me he just had a troubling call from a woman he'd been seeing. He admitted he'd been having an affair with Rochelle Salazar. She called to tell him she had something she needed to do this afternoon, and now that his wife was dead they were free to live together just like he'd told her he wanted to. Then she went on to tell him she knew how unhappy he'd been in his marriage, and she'd taken care of it for him."

"Wow! That's kind of like admitting she did it."

"That's not all. She said she wanted to pick him up when he got off work today and drive across the country to someplace where they could start a new life together. He said he never got a chance to answer because she said she had to go, and she'd see him later."

"Sounds to me like our plan is going to work," Kat said.

"I certainly hope so. Two other police officers and I will be outside the front door from the time you enter the clinic. You promised Blaine you'd have Rudy with you. How are you going to handle that?"

"I think it would set off Rochelle's radar if I took him into the treatment room with me. I'll leave him in the reception area and tell her I had to take him to the vet before I came, and I didn't want to leave him in the car during my treatment, because it was too hot for him to stay in the car."

"That sounds good. You have the wire I gave you, and you'll be wearing it, right?"

"Yes, and you'll be able to hear everything she says to me."

"I called Dr. Green a little while ago and reminded her not to touch the needle box. She said Rochelle told her she was going home for lunch, because she was afraid she'd left the stove on. Let's talk about Rudy for a minute. Mr. Evans said he was highly trained and will obey both hand signals and verbal commands. If we need his help, is there something I should say?"

"No, what I plan on doing is looking out the door of the treatment room so I can see what Rochelle's doing as soon as Dr. Green enters the room. Depending on what happens, I'll either give Rudy a hand signal or yell a command if it's needed. By the way, there's a back door behind the reception counter that leads to the parking lot reserved for doctors. Several buildings share it. You might want to have one of your policemen outside that door."

"That I didn't know. Thanks, and I definitely will. Think that's about it. Good luck, and I'll see you this afternoon."

*****

At 4:00 that afternoon Kat opened the clinic door and she and Rudy walked in. "Good afternoon, Rochelle. I brought my dog, Rudy, with me because he had a check-up at the vet this afternoon and they were running late, so I didn't have time to take him home before my appointment. It's so hot out I can't leave him in the car. He won't be any trouble. He's very well-behaved, and he'll just lie down here and wait for me."

"That's fine. If you're ready, I'll show you to your treatment room. You're in room number three. Please follow me."

Kat told Rudy to stay, and she walked down the hall to room number three, sure that Rochelle could hear her wildly beating heart. She steeled herself not to look at the needle box while Rochelle spread the roll of sanitary paper on the treatment table that she changed for each new patient. "There you go. For this treatment you'll be on your back. Just get comfortable, and Dr. Green will be with you shortly. You might even be able to take a little nap during your treatment." Kat sat down on the table and Rochelle walked out of the room, leaving the door ajar.

As soon as she left Kat stood up and looked in the needle box. There were only eight needles, and that's the number of needles the article on the flash drive had indicated were needed for the treatment of depression. Kat shivered involuntarily.

There was a knock on the door and Kat said, "Come in."

Dr. Green entered the room and winked at Kat. She closed the door and then softly reopened it just a crack. Kat walked over to the door and peeked around the corner. She heard Rochelle slam a drawer shut in her desk and swear. She saw Rochelle open the drawer again and begin frantically pulling things out of it. The drawer Rochelle was pulling things out of was the drawer where Mitzi had found the flash drive.

Kat motioned for Mitzi to come closer so she could whisper in her ear and at the same time whisper into the wire, "I'm sure she's looking for the flash drive Mitzi took out of the drawer. Now she's got her purse, and she took her keys out of it. She looks like she's come unhinged. She's turning towards the back door. She's opening it. It's jammed." Kat raised her head from where she'd been speaking into the wire and yelled, "Rudy, attack!"

At that moment, the front door flew open, and Detective Shafer and one of his men as well as Blaine rushed into the room. At the same time, Rudy jumped over the counter and pinned Rochelle to the back wall of the reception room. The back door opened and another policeman came in. All of them had their guns drawn. Dr. Green and Kat rushed down the hall and joined them.

"Get this stupid dog off me. He's going to bite me. Get him off!" Rochelle yelled.

"Rudy, stand down. Come."

The big Rottweiler looked at Rochelle, let out a low deep growl, and then walked over to where Kat was standing. She gave him a hand signal indicating he was to sit. One policeman subdued Rochelle while the other one handcuffed her.

"Which one is room three?" Detective Shafer asked. "I want to close the door so nothing gets disturbed. I'm treating it as a crime scene, and it's off limits to everyone. No exceptions. I told my fingerprint expert to be on standby. I'll give him a call. He turned to

Rochelle. "Mrs. Salazar, I'm not charging you with anything at the moment, but if your fingerprints are found on the acupuncture needles, and if there's poison on the tips of those needles, I will be charging you with the murder of Sandy Hendrick and the attempted murder of Mrs. Denham. I think we have enough evidence along with what Matt Hendrick told me to make sure you spend a long, long time in prison."

"Matt told you I called? How could he? I killed Sandy, so he and I could be together, just like he wanted."

"Mrs. Denham, I assume you still have that wire on, and if you do, we now have a full confession on tape. If not, there are enough of us here who heard what she said, so I feel certain it will stand up in court. Yes, Mrs. Salazar, you definitely are going to prison for a long time. You're under arrest for murdering Sandy Hendrick. By law I need to read you your Miranda rights. Depending on what we find, extra charges will probably be added. Nick, Don, take her in."

Blaine walked over to Kat and said, "Are you all right?"

"I'm fine, but I have to admit I was a little nervous thinking Rochelle might decide to take one of those needles and plunge it into me. My heart's beating a mile a minute, and my blood pressure is probably sky high. Maybe I need a treatment for that," she said laughing. "Now I've got a question for you. What are you doing here? That wasn't part of the plan."

"Maybe it wasn't for you, but I knew from the moment you came up with this sting plan of yours, I was going to be here. My day has been a waste. I couldn't do anything but think about what could go wrong with your plan. Believe me, I'm just as glad as I'm sure you are that this is over."

The office phone rang and Dr. Green said, "I'll get it," as she walked into her office.

A few minutes later Detective Shafer and his fingerprint expert walked out of room three carrying bags of what Kat presumed was evidence. "Mrs. Denham, the department is very indebted to you for what you did today. Somehow, I feel we're going to be reading about this in a book. Would I be right?" he asked laughing.

"Yes, when I get my beating heart and blood pressure under control, I'll probably start writing it. Thanks for believing in me. I know you had your doubts in the beginning."

"My job is to doubt everyone and everything. Think it's kind of ironic that the district attorney will probably be charging Mrs. Salazar with murder, and he was here when she confessed. Mrs. Denham, you have to admit that is stranger than fiction." As he walked out the door he turned and gave her a mock salute. "A bit of advice, Mrs. Denham. Maybe it would be better to go back to writing your steamy novels instead of murder mysteries if you're going to be personally involved in them. Think Mr. Evans would agree."

"You've got that right," Blaine said.

Blaine turned to Kat, "Well, now that we don't have to worry about solving a murder mystery, it's time to start planning a couple of weddings…"

He was interrupted by a scream of glee coming from Dr. Green's office. They looked at each other in surprise, as she opened her door and screamed again. "Woo Hoo! You are looking at the new Assistant Dean of the Department of Acupuncture."

"Congratulations! I assume that's what the call was about," Kat said.

"Yes. Another case of strange coincidences. Dr. Nguyen went to Dr. Warren's office this afternoon unannounced. He told him he needed to talk to him. I won't bore you with all the details, but the bottom line is he's leaving tonight for Vietnam to visit his ailing father, and he's accepted a position as an acupuncturist in Hong Kong. His wife is staying here and making the arrangements for their move." Mitzi said.

She continued, "I probably should ask Detective Shafer to have his computer expert search both Rochelle's computer and Dr. Nguyen's to see if the information that was on the flash drive is on either one of their computers. He said he'd give me a call after they did a preliminary search for fingerprints and poison. I'll tell him then. I imagine that would be part of his case against Rochelle."

Kat turned to Blaine, "Let's go plan weddings. I cook when I'm nervous, so you're going to get a very good dinner tonight."

"I've learned to stay away from cooking when I get nervous," Mitzi said laughing, "I eat out, and tonight I think I'll treat Rex to the best dinner in town. It's a night for a real celebration. Talk to you later, I need to call him and tell him what's happened. I have three messages from him as it is. He's probably a nervous wreck," she said as she walked back into her office.

As Kat and Blaine walked to their cars, Rudy right next to Kat, he said, "Okay, what are we having for this fine dinner?"

"How does beef wellington sound accompanied by fingerling potatoes and a fresh green salad? For dessert I made mini-cheesecakes, and I'll serve them with that Italian liqueur, limoncello, and they'll be topped with vanilla ice cream."

"How does that sound? Are you crazy? What's not to like about that? We should have a murder mystery solved every day if it means we get to eat like that."

"I don't think so, but now that it's behind us, I have something to ask you."

"I'm all ears."

"I was thinking maybe you should spend the night. In addition to Mitzi and Rex's wedding, I'd like to get started on ours."

"Lady, your wish is my command, and I doubt that I have to tell you how long I've been looking forward to this."

"Yeah, me too," Kat said smiling.

*****

They'd just finished the cheesecakes and limoncello when Kat's phone rang. "I'd almost rather you didn't answer it," Blaine said, "but let me assure you I'm staying, no matter what's on the other end of that call."

"Agreed. Oh, it's Detective Shafer. Maybe he has some news." She picked up her phone and answered it. "Good evening, Detective. Did you find out anything?" she asked.

He started to talk and she interrupted him, saying, "Let me put you on speakerphone. I know Blaine's as anxious as I am to hear what you've found out."

"Okay," Detective Shafter began, "we were able to get quite a bit done in a rather short period of time. My computer expert did examine Dr. Nguyen's computer and found the same information that was on Rochelle's flash drive, at least we presume it was hers, but I guess we'll never know what he was going to do with it, if anything. We took a statement from Matt Hendrick regarding Mrs. Salazar's statement that she'd taken care of the situation with his wife."

"That just has the most ominous ring to it," Kat said.

"I know," he said, "but here's where the money is. The only fingerprints on the needles in the box we recovered from treatment room number three were those of Rochelle Salazar, and there was Digoxin on each of the needle tips. Our expert said there was enough poison there to kill several people. Along with her confession, we have a very good case against her. She's also been charged with attempted murder. She said something I've never encountered before. She plans on entering a guilty plea at her arraignment, so she can avoid a trial. Mrs. Salazar said she loves Matt Hendrick so much she doesn't want to embarrass him. Can you believe it? She wants to protect a guy that plays around like he does? People never fail to amaze me."

"Me, too. Well, I guess that's the end of it. Thanks for everything."

"The only thing that might happen is she might change her plea, and it could go to trial. If that happens, you'll have to testify."

"No problem. Happy to do my civic duty. Have a good weekend, Detective."

"You too."

After Kat ended the call, she turned to Blaine and said, "Well, that's that. Glad you called Nick and told him what happened. I think it's over. What a week."

Blaine walked over to her and gently put his arms around her. "Kat, it's time. No more distractions."

CHAPTER TWENTY-SIX

Although the summer had been exceptionally hot, even for Kansas, it was as if the wedding gods were smiling down on Mitzi and Rex. At 5:00 in the afternoon, thirty minutes before they were to be married, the temperature was a comfortable seventy degrees. Kat and her gardener had put a lot of work in on her back yard, and it was a beautiful riot of colors. Her yard backed up to an urban forest of deep green trees which set off the white latticework arch where Mitzi and Rex were going to stand and say their vows.

The guests had been greeted and seated, and just before Kat was getting ready to walk down the aisle as the matron of honor, Lacie whispered to her, "Mom, you look beautiful. This is so exciting, kind of a dress rehearsal for your wedding."

"Thanks, honey, but after the last two months I think I'm going to be happy we decided to have it at the country club. What started out as planting a few new flowers, getting a couple of new appliances, some throw pillows, and hardware for the doors turned out be nothing short of a major redecorating job. The only thing I can think of that we didn't do was tear down some walls," she said laughing.

Blaine chimed in, "Kat, the house looks fabulous. Now we won't have to do anything for years."

"Blaine, you had some great ideas," Lacie said, "and I'm glad I had some backup from you on some of mine. Mom's a little reluctant to spend money, but that doesn't seem to be a problem with you," Lacie said.

"Quick, go take your seats," Kat said. "It's almost time, and as long as Rex and Mitzi have waited to get married, I want it to be perfect."

The music started and Kat walked down the aisle, beautiful in a pale apricot cocktail suit. She smiled broadly at Rex and his medical partner, Lou, who was serving as his best man. She turned to face the guests, as the music switched to "Here Comes the Bride," and a glowing Mitzi slowly walked down the aisle, her eyes locked on Rex. Everybody loves a happy ever after story, and most of the guests had tears in their eyes or on their cheeks as they watched the happy couple exchange their vows.

Kat and Blaine smiled at each other, knowing that soon, they too would be saying their vows. Mid-life romance, thank you, was alive and well in the small Kansas university town!

RECIPES

ORANGE BALSAMIC LAMB CHOPS

Ingredients:
4 tsp. extra virgin olive oil, divided (You'll see a lot written about extra virgin olive oil vs. regular, but when I'm doing a salad dressing or a marinade, I think extra virgin is better.)
2 tsps. grated orange rind
1 tbsp. fresh orange juice
8 (4 oz.) lamb chops, trimmed (I usually buy a rack of lamb, cut them into individual chops, and trim them myself.)
1 tsp. kosher salt (And yes, I do prefer kosher salt for most kinds of cooking when fine salt isn't called for. Think it gives the dish more flavor - a major source of disagreement in the Harman kitchen depending on whether I'm cooking or my husband is!)
½ tsp freshly ground pepper (Believe me, it's worth the extra effort.)
3 tbsps. balsamic vinegar
Cooking spray

Directions:
Combine 3 tsp. olive oil, orange rind, and juice and put into a large zip-lock bag along with the lamb chops. Coat well. Let it stand at room temperature for 10 minutes. Heat a large grill pan over

medium-high heat. Coat pan with cooking spray. When hot, add the lamb chops to the pan and cook 2 minutes per side medium rare, longer for medium or well done. (If the lamb chops are of different thicknesses, put the thickest ones on first and cook for about a minute longer. You may have to adjust more than that if there is a wide variation.)

While the lamb is cooking, put the vinegar in a small saucepan over medium-high heat and bring to a boil to reduce it. Cook 3 minutes or until the vinegar is syrupy. Mix the remaining 1 teaspoon olive oil with the vinegar and drizzle over the lamb chops. Enjoy!

COLD TROUT CUCUMBER SALAD WITH CREAMY YOGURT DRESSING

Ingredients:
2 whole trout (Believe it or not, a lot of supermarkets do carry whole trout!)
½ head red leaf lettuce, shredded
½ head iceberg lettuce, shredded
½ cucumber, peeled, halved lengthwise, and thinly cut crosswise
4 Roma tomatoes, quartered lengthwise (If you can't find them, you can use another kind of tomato.)
1 avocado, peeled and sliced into bite-size pieces (about ¾")
½ red onion – slice the rings into bite-size pieces (about ¾")
8 mushrooms, quartered with stems removed
¼ cup sliced almonds, lightly toasted in a frying pan for 3-4 minutes
¼ cup pine nuts, lightly toasted in a frying pan for 3-4 minutes
½ cup creamy yogurt dressing (I use Boathouse Farms Cilantro Avocado, but if you can't find it, look for something similar.)
Lemon pepper for garnish (I use Lawry's, but again, if you can't find it, look for something similar.)
Oil spray

Directions:

Trout: Preheat oven to 400 degrees. Remove the heads and tails with a cleaver and discard (If you're like me, this is where husbands or significant others come in handy!) Place trout in a slightly oiled ovenproof dish and bake for 20 minutes. Remove from oven and place trout on a plate and chill in refrigerator for at least one hour. Place chilled trout on a cutting board, and with your fingers, peel off the skin on both sides and discard.

With a sharp thin knife or a spatula scrape away and discard the dark material under the skin that runs down the center on both sides so you end up with clean white meat. Slide the knife along the backbone, separate the top filet from the backbone, and set aside. Starting at the head end, gently lift the backbone from the bottom filet and discard. Remove and discard the fins and any small bones not removed when the backbone's removed. Return the boneless filets to the plate and refrigerate until ready to assemble the salad. (I know it sounds complicated, but it's not, trust me!)

Salad: Place all ingredients with the exception of the toasted nuts in a large bowl and gently toss while adding the dressing. Place dressed salad equally on 4 serving plates and sprinkle with toasted nuts. Sprinkle lemon pepper on each trout filet and place one filet on top of each salad. Serve additional dressing on the side in case more is desired. Enjoy!

NOTE: I recommend you prepare the trout several hours in advance. The filets are quite delicate and break apart easily. When transferring them to or from the refrigerator, use a long thin spatula and "scoop" each filet up lengthwise by sliding the spatula gently under the filet, starting at the thickest end.

BEEF WELLINGTON

Ingredients:

1 center cut beef tenderloin about 8 inches long and 2 ½ lbs., trimmed

4 tbsp. butter
2 lbs. cremini mushrooms finely chopped in a food processor (If you can't find cremini, don't worry about it. Plain white mushrooms work just as well.)
1 lb. frozen puff pastry (You can easily find this at the supermarket.) Thaw in refrigerator.
¼ cup flour
1 egg, beaten
½ tsp. kosher salt, divided
½ tsp. freshly ground black pepper, divided

Directions:

Preheat oven to 425 degrees. Sprinkle ¼ tsp. salt and ¼ tsp. pepper on beef surface. In a large skillet over high heat, melt butter. When it foams, add a handful of the mushrooms. Cook for 1 minute. Repeat until all of the mushrooms have been sautéed or until the liquid they release evaporates and they're brown. Season with remaining salt and pepper and set aside to cool.

Sprinkle a sheet pan with cold water. Scatter the flour on a wooden surface and roll pastry dough into a rectangle large enough to completely wrap around the tenderloin. Evenly spread the cooled mushrooms over the dough. Place the beef along one long edge of the dough and roll the meat up in the dough so it's completely enclosed in the dough. Place the wrapped beef on the sheet pan, seam side down. Seal each end by folding it under the beef.

Using a thin sharp knife, make a series of diagonal slashes into the dough across the top. (Don't cut into the meat when you're doing this.) Brush the top of the dough with the beaten egg. Bake for about 40 minutes or until the pastry is golden brown. (You might want to use a meat thermometer as ovens vary. For rare, 120 degrees, medium, 125 degrees. Keep in mind that the temperature will rise another 5 degrees while the roast rests.)

Transfer the roast to a serving platter and lightly cover it. Let it rest about 10 minutes. (I usually use loose tin foil or paper towels.) Use a sharp knife and cut pieces approximately 1" thick. You can plate it or let people serve themselves. Enjoy!

OSSO BUCO

Ingredients:
3 veal shanks, about 1 lb. each, trimmed
2 sprigs fresh rosemary
2 sprigs fresh thyme
4 tbsps. fresh parsley, chopped
1 tbsp. lemon zest
1 dry bay leaf
3 whole cloves
½ tsp. kosher salt, divided
¼ tsp. freshly ground black pepper
Flour, for dredging
½ cup vegetable oil
1 small onion, diced
1 small carrot, diced
1 stalk celery, diced (I use one from the center because I think it's more tender.)
1 tbsp. tomato paste (You can use canned or one that comes in a tube – I prefer the tube, because it seems every time I buy a can, I end up throwing the unused portion of it out.)
1 cup dry white wine
3 cups chicken stock (If you don't have homemade, and most of us don't, you can make your own from cubes or Wyler's – think it's a lot cheaper than buying it in a can or box.)
Cheesecloth
Kitchen twine

Directions:
Put the rosemary, thyme, bay leaves, and cloves in the cheesecloth to make a bouquet garni. Tie it off with the twine.

Pat the veal shanks dry with paper towels to remove excess moisture. Secure the meat to the bone by tying each one with the kitchen twine. Season with salt and pepper. Dredge the shanks in flour, shaking off the excess flour.

In a large Dutch oven pot, heat the oil on medium-high until it smokes. Add the veal shanks and brown on all sides, about 3 minutes per side. Remove and put on a metal tray. Reduce the heat to medium and add the onion, carrot, and celery. Sprinkle with the remaining salt to draw out the moisture. Sauté until soft, about 7 – 9 minutes. Add the tomato paste and mix well.

Add the veal shanks and the wine. Simmer over medium heat until the wine is reduced by half. Add the bouquet garni and 2 cups of the chicken stock. Bring to a boil, then reduce the heat to low, cover the pan, and simmer for 1 ½ hours. Check every 20 minutes and add additional chicken stock as needed so the liquid remains about ¾ of the way up the shanks.

Remove shanks and place on serving platter. Cut off the twine and discard. Remove bouquet garni. Pour the juice and sauce over the shanks and garnish with lemon zest and parsley. Enjoy!

KAT'S LITTLE LEMON CHEESECAKES

Ingredients:
2/3 cup sugar
1/2 cup lemon juice
4 tsps. finely grated lemon peel
 Two 8 oz. packages of cream cheese at room temperature
1 cup whole milk ricotta cheese
2 extra-large or jumbo eggs (I prefer jumbo.)
1/2 cup lemon curd (I buy it ready-made at the supermarket.)
Nonstick vegetable oil spray

Directions:
Preheat oven to 425 degrees. Spray 8 ramekins or custard cups with the spray. Beat sugar, lemon juice, and lemon peel in a large bowl until the sugar dissolves. Add softened cream cheese and ricotta cheese and beat until smooth. Add eggs and beat until well-blended.

Divide the batter among the prepared cups and place on a baking sheet. Bake for about 18 minutes or until puffed, set in center, and golden brown. Chill in the refrigerator for at least two hours. Enjoy!

NOTE: I like to serve this with the Italian liqueur, limoncello, and top the cheesecake with a dollop of vanilla ice cream.

Kindle & Ebooks for FREE

Go to www.dianneharman.com/freepaperback.html and get your FREE copies of Dianne's books and Dianne's favorite recipes immediately by signing up for her newsletter.

Once you've signed up for her newsletter you're eligible to win a Kindle. One lucky winner is picked every week. Hurry before the offer ends!

ABOUT THE AUTHOR

Dianne lives in Huntington Beach, California, with her husband, Tom, a former California State Senator, and her boxer dog, Kelly. Her passions are cooking, reading, and dogs, so whenever she has a little free time, you can either find her in the kitchen, playing with Kelly in the back yard, or curled up with the latest book she's reading.

Her award winning books include:

Cedar Bay Cozy Mystery Series
Kelly's Koffee Shop, Murder at Jade Cove, White Cloud Retreat, Marriage and Murder, Murder in the Pearl District, Murder in Calico Gold, Murder at the Cooking School, Murder in Cuba, Trouble at the Kennel, Murder on the East Coast

Liz Lucas Cozy Mystery Series
Murder in Cottage #6, Murder & Brandy Boy, The Death Card, Murder at The Bed & Breakfast, The Blue Butterfly, Murder at the Big T Lodge

High Desert Cozy Mystery Series
Murder & The Monkey Band, Murder & The Secret Cave, Murdered by Country Music

Midwest Cozy Mystery Series
Murdered by Words, Murder at the Clinic

Jack Trout Cozy Mystery Series
Murdered in Argentina

Coyote Series
Blue Coyote Motel, Coyote in Provence, Cornered Coyote

Website: www.dianneharman.com
Blog: www.dianneharman.com/blog
Email: dianne@dianneharman.com

Newsletter
If you would like to be notified of her latest releases please go to www.dianneharman.com and sign up for her newsletter.

Made in United States
North Haven, CT
20 November 2021

11297655R00093